THE JUNIOR GREAT

DISCUSSION PROGRAM

JUNIOR GREAT BOOKS

A Program of Interpretive Reading
and Discussion

Series Seven, Volume Two

EDITED BY

Richard P. Dennis and Edwin P. Moldof

THE GREAT BOOKS FOUNDATION

published and distributed by

THE GREAT BOOKS FOUNDATION
a nonprofit corporation
307 North Michigan Avenue,
Chicago, Illinois 60601

5

ACKNOWLEDGMENTS

The Great Books Foundation wishes to thank the following publishers, authors and literary agencies for permission to reprint the material in this Junior Great Books series:

Delacorte Press/Seymour Lawrence for "Harrison Bergeron," copyright © 1961 by Kurt Vonnegut, Jr. Originally published in *Fantasy and Science Fiction Magazine.* Reprinted from the book, WELCOME TO THE MONKEY HOUSE, by Kurt Vonnegut, Jr.

Doubleday & Company, Inc., for "The Evildoer," reprinted from SHADOWS AND LIGHT, by Anton Chekhov, translated by Miriam Morton, copyright 1968.

Farrar, Straus & Giroux, Inc. for "The Zodiacs," from CORKY'S BROTHER by Jay Neugeboren, copyright © 1966.

Grosset & Dunlap, Inc., New York, for "Rufus," from a DEATH IN THE FAMILY, by James Agee, copyright © 1957 by the James Agee Trust.

Harper's Magazine for "Univac to Univac," by Louis B. Salomon. Copyright © 1958 by *Harper's Magazine,* reprinted from the March 1958 issue.

The New American Library of World Literature, New York, for "The Overcoat," from THE DIARY OF A MADMAN AND OTHER STORIES by Nikolai Gogol, translated by Andrew McAndrew, copyright © 1960.

Penguin Books Ltd., for "The Companion," by Yevgeny Yevtushenko, from YEVTUSHENKO: SELECTED POEMS translated by Robin Milner-Gulland and Peter Levi, S. J., copyright © 1962.

William Saroyan for "Gaston," copyright © 1962, by The Atlantic Monthly Company, Boston.

Sterling Lord Agency, Inc. for "The Gun Without a Bang," copyright © 1958 by Robert Sheckley.

Toni Strassman, Authors' representative, for "The Stone Boy," by Gina Berriault. First published in *Mademoiselle* in 1957. Copyright 1957 by Gina Berriault.

CONTENTS

THE EVILDOER

BEFORE THE investigating magistrate stood an emaciated little peasant in a striped shirt made of ticking and in patched trousers. His hairy face, covered with smallpox scars, and his eyes, scarcely visible under thick overhanging brows, bore an expression of surly coarseness. His head was overgrown with a thicket of long, uncombed hair, giving him the air of a cross spider. He was barefoot.

"Denis Grigoryev," the investigating magistrate began, "step up and answer my questions: On the seventh day of the present month of July, the railroad watchman Ivan Semyonov Akinfov, checking the rails on that morning, caught you at the one hundred and forty-first milepost unscrewing the nut of one of the bolts that fasten the rails to the ties. Here is the nut. With said nut he detained you. Is that correct?"

"What d'ye say?"

"Did all that take place as described by Akinfov?"

"Yes, it was so."

"Very well. Tell me, then, why did you unscrew the nut?"

"What d'ye say?"

"Never mind the 'what-d'ye-says' and answer my question: Why did you unscrew the nut?"

"If I hadn't needed it, I'd not have unscrewed it," Denis muttered throatily, with a furtive glance at the ceiling.

"For what purpose did you need it all of a sudden?"

"The nut?... We make sinkers out of the nuts."

"And who is 'we'?"

"Us, the common folk—the Klimovo peasants, that is..."

"Listen, don't you play the fool with me and talk sense. It won't do you any good to lie to me about sinkers!"

1

"I've never lied in my life, so why would I start lying now?'' Denis grumbled, blinking. "Can it be, Your Honor, that you believe one can fish *without* sinkers? If you cast live bait or worms on a fishhook, would it go down to the bottom without a sinker?... And you say *I'm* lying...'' Denis smirked. "What the devil is the use of live bait if it is going to float on the surface! The perch, the pike, and the eel are always on the bottom, and if the bait floats on the water it will only catch a bullhead and only once in a while at that. Besides, there are no bullheads in our river—this fish likes lots of room...''

"Why are you bothering me about bullheads?''

"What d'ye say? Didn't you ask me yourself?... Around here even the gentry catch fish that way. Even the smallest urchin wouldn't think of fishing without a sinker. Of course, someone with no sense at all might try it without a sinker— rules aren't made for fools... ''

"So, you state that you unscrewed this nut in order to use it as a sinker?''

"What else? Not to play knucklebones with!''

"But you could have used a piece of lead, or a bullet, or some kind of nail... ''

"You don't find lead lying around to be picked up, you have to buy it, and a nail's no good. There's nothing better than a nut. It's heavy and it's got a hole.''

"He keeps acting the fool! You might think he was born yesterday or dropped out of the sky! Can't you get it through your thick skull what all this unscrewing can lead to? If not for the watchman, the train might have gone off the rails, people might have been killed! You would have killed these people.''

"God forbid, Your Honor! Why would I want to kill people? Am I not a Christian—am I some kind of criminal? Praise be to God, my good sir, I've lived all my life not only without killing but without even thinking of such a thing. Save us and have mercy upon us, Queen of Heaven!—how can you even say such a thing?''

"And, according to you, what causes train wrecks? Unscrew two or three nuts and you'll have a train wreck!''

The peasant smirked and screwed up his eyes at the investigating magistrate, expressing disbelief.

"You don't say! How many years have all of us here in the village been unscrewing those nuts and, the Lord protect us!—there've been no wrecks, no people killed. Now, if I'd carried off a rail or, let's suppose, if I'd put a log in the way—then, maybe, the train might've gone off the track... but, pfft! just a nut!''

"Do try to get it through your head that nuts hold the rails fast to the ties!''

"We understand that... You'd think we go around unscrewing all of them—the way you talk. We leave lots of them. We don't do it without using common sense... we understand... '' And Denis yawned and made the sign of the cross over his mouth.

"Last year a train went off the rails here,'' said the magistrate. "Now it's clear why!''

"Forgive me... I didn't quite hear what you said...''

"I say, it's clear now why there was a train wreck here last year... I now understand the cause.''

"That's why you've been given a good education—all of you, our benefactors—to understand... The Lord knows to whom to give understanding... You've figured it out properly, but the watchman—a mere peasant like the rest of us, without a brain in his head—grabs me by the scruff of the neck and pulls me in! Yes, as the saying goes: a peasant has the brain of a peasant. Write down also, Your Honor, that he punched me twice in the teeth and once in the chest.''

"When your place was searched they found a second nut. Where and when did you unscrew that one?"

"Are you asking about the nut that was hidden under the little red trunk?"

"I have no idea where you hid it, but it was found! When did you unscrew that one?"

"I didn't unscrew it: Ignashka, one-eyed Semyon's sonny, did it for me. I'm talking now about the one under the little trunk, you know, but the other one, the one in the sled outside, in the yard, that one I unscrewed together with Mitrofan."

"Which Mitrofan?"

"With Mitrofan Petrov. Haven't you heard of him? He makes fishnets—sells them to the gentry. He uses many of these nuts: about ten for each net... "

"Now, listen. Article 1081 of the Penal Code stipulates that every deliberate damage done to a railroad endangering the transportation along said railroad, and when the accused knows that said damage would result in a disaster—you understand?... *knows!* ... and you couldn't help knowing what this unscrewing would lead to... the accused is punishable by banishment and convict labor."

"Of course, you know best! We are ignorant folk—what do we understand?"

"You understand very well what this is all about! You are lying... you are faking!"

"Why should I lie? Ask anyone in the village if you don't believe me. Only bleak is caught without a sinker, and a minnow is hardly a fish at all, and even that you can't catch without a sinker."

"Yes, yes, and what about the bullhead?" prompted the magistrate with a mocking smile.

"We haven't got bullheads in our parts. If we cast our lines without a sinker on the surface, with a butterfly as bait, all we get is mullet, and even that only once in a while.''

"That's enough of that! Be quiet!''

There was silence. Denis shifted his weight from one foot to the other, stared at the table covered with a green cloth, and screwed up his eyes as though he was looking not at the cloth but at the sun. The investigating magistrate was writing rapidly.

"Can I go now?'' Denis asked after a brief silence.

"No. I must place you in custody and send you to prison.''

Denis opened his eyes wide and, raising his heavy eyebrows, looked inquiringly at the magistrate: "What d'ye mean—to prison?! Your Honor, I haven't the time for that; I must go to the fair to collect three rubles from Egor—for lard . . . ''

"Be quiet! Don't interrupt!''

"To prison! . . . At least if I'd done something . . . all right . . . I'd go. But to be sent to prison for nothing . . . I live a clean life . . . why send me to prison? I didn't steal anything, and as far as I know I've never started a brawl . . . but if you have doubts about those tax arrears—don't believe a word the village elder says . . . ask the permanent member of the village commons—he's no Christian, that elder! . . . ''

"Be quiet!''

"I've been quiet enough,'' muttered Denis, "but that elder . . . whatever lies he's told about the assessment . . . I'd take an oath . . . there are three of us brothers: Kuz'ma Grigoryev, then Egor Grigoryev, and then there's me, Denis Grigoryev . . . ''

"You're interfering! Hey, there, Semyon,'' cried the magistrate, "take him out!''

" . . . we're three brothers . . . ,'' grumbled Denis as two husky soldiers seized him and led him out of the room. "One brother is not another's keeper... Kuz'ma doesn't pay, then it's me, Denis, who must answer for him... some judges! Too bad he's dead, our late master, the General— may he rest in the Kingdom of Heaven!—or he'd show you judges... you must know what you're about before you judge and not do it just like that... it's all right even to flog a man... but for an evil deed... justly..."

RUFUS

WHEN BREAKFAST was over he wandered listlessly into the sitting room and looked all around, but he did not see any place where he would like to sit down. He felt deeply idle and empty and at the same time gravely exhilarated, as if this were the morning of his birthday, except that this day seemed even more particularly his own day. There was nothing in the way it looked which was not ordinary, but it was filled with a noiseless and invisible kind of energy. He could see his mother's face while she told them about it and hear her voice, over and over, and silently, over and over, while he looked around the sitting room and through the window into the street, words repeated themselves, He's dead. He died last night while I was asleep and now it was already morning. He has already been dead since way last night and I didn't even know until I woke up. He has been dead all night while I was asleep and now it is morning and I am awake but he is still dead and he will stay right on being dead all afternoon and all night and all tomorrow while I am asleep again and wake up again and go to sleep again and he can't come back home again ever any more but I will see him once more before he is taken away. Dead now. He died last night while I was asleep and now it is already morning.

A boy went by with his books in a strap.

Two girls went by with their satchels.

He went to the hat rack and took his satchel and his hat and started back down the hall to the kitchen to get his lunch; then he remembered his new cap. But it was upstairs. It would be in Mama's and Daddy's room, he could remember when she took it off his head. He did not want to go in for it where she was lying down and now he realized, too, that he did not want

7

to wear it. He would like to tell her good-bye before he went to school, but he did not want to go in and see her lying down and looking like that. He kept on towards the kitchen. He would tell Aunt Hannah good-bye instead.

She was at the sink washing dishes and Catherine sat on a kitchen chair watching her. He looked all around but he could not see any lunch. I guess she doesn't know about lunch, he reflected. She did not seem to realize that he was there so, after a moment, he said, "Good-bye."

"What-*is*-it?" she said and turned her lowered head, peering. "Why, Rufus!" she exclaimed, in such a tone that he wondered what he had done. "You're not going to *school*," she said, and now he realized that she was not mad at him.

"I can stay out of school?"

"Of course you can. You must. Today and tomorrow as well and—for a sufficient time. A few days. Now put up your things, and stay right in this house, child."

He looked at her and said to himself: but then they can't see me; but he knew there was no use begging her; already she was busy with the dishes again.

He went back along the hall towards the hat rack. In the first moment he had been only surprised and exhilarated not to have to go to school, and something of this sense of privilege remained, but almost immediately he was also disappointed. He could now see vividly how they would all look up when he came into the schoolroom and how the teacher would say something nice about his father and about him, and he knew that on this day everybody would treat him well, and even look up to him, for something had happened to him today which had not happened to any other boy in school, any other boy in town. They might even give him part of their lunches.

He felt even more profoundly empty and idle than before.

He laid down his satchel on the seat of the hat rack, but he kept his hat on. She'll spank me, he thought. Even worse, he could foresee her particular, crackling kind of anger. I won't let her find out, he told himself. Taking great care to be silent, he let himself out the front door.

The air was cool and gray and here and there along the street, shapeless and watery sunlight strayed and vanished. Now that he was in this outdoor air he felt even more listless and powerful; he was alone, and the silent, invisible energy was everywhere. He stood on the porch and supposed that everyone he saw passing knew of an event so famous. A man was walking quickly up the street and as Rufus watched him, and waited for the man to meet his eyes, he felt a great quiet lifting within him of pride and shyness, and he felt his face break into a smile, and then an uncontrollable grin, which he knew he must try to make sober again; but the man walked past without looking at him, and so did the next man who walked past in the other direction. Two schoolboys passed whose faces he knew, so he knew that they must know his, but they did not even seem to see him. Arthur and Alvin Tripp came down their front steps and along the far sidewalk and now he was sure, and came down his own front steps and halfway out to the sidewalk, but then he stopped, for now, although both of them looked across into his eyes, and he into theirs, they did not cross the street to him or even say hello, but kept on their way, still looking into his eyes with a kind of shy curiosity, even when their heads were turned almost backwards on their necks, and he turned his own head slowly, watching them go by, but when he saw that they were not going to speak he took care not to speak either.

What's the matter with them, he wondered, and still watched them; and even now, far down the street, Arthur kept turning his head, and for several steps Alvin walked backwards.

What are they mad about?

Now they no longer looked around, and now he watched them vanish under the hill.

Maybe they don't know, he thought. Maybe the others don't know, either.

He came out to the sidewalk.

Maybe everybody knew. Or maybe he knew something of great importance which nobody else knew. The alternatives were not at all distinct in his mind; he was puzzled, but no less proud and expectant than before. My daddy's dead, he said to himself slowly, and then, shyly, he said it aloud: "My daddy's dead." Nobody in sight seemed to have heard; he had said it to nobody in particular. "My daddy's dead," he said again, chiefly for his own benefit. It sounded powerful, solid, and entirely creditable, and he knew that if need be he would tell people. He watched a large, slow man come towards him and waited for the man to look at him and acknowledge the fact first, but when the man was just ahead of him, and still did not appear even to have seen him, he told him, "My daddy's dead," but the man did not seem to hear him, he just swung on by. He took care to tell the next man sooner and the man's face looked almost as if he were dodging a blow but he went on by, looking back a few steps later with a worried face; and after a few steps more he turned and came slowly back.

"What was that you said, sonny?" he asked; he was frowning slightly.

"My daddy's dead," Rufus said, expectantly.

"You mean that sure enough?" the man asked.

"He died last night when I was asleep and now he can't come home ever any more."

The man looked at him as if something hurt him.

"Where do you live, sonny?"

"Right here"; he showed with his eyes.

"Do your folks know you out here wandern round?"

He felt his stomach go empty. He looked frankly into his eyes and nodded quickly.

The man just looked at him and Rufus realized: He doesn't believe me. How do they always know?

"You better just go on back in the house, son," he said. "They won't like you being out here on the street." He kept looking at him, hard.

Rufus looked into his eyes with reproach and apprehension, and turned in at his walk. The man still stood there. Rufus went on slowly up his steps, and looked around. The man was on his way again but at the moment Rufus looked around, he did too, and now he stopped again.

He shook his head and said, in a friendly voice which made Rufus feel ashamed. "How would your daddy like it, you out here telling strangers how he's dead?"

Rufus opened the door, taking care not to make a sound, and stepped in and silently closed it, and hurried into the sitting room. Through the curtains he watched the man. He still stood there, lighting a cigarette, but now he started walking again. He looked back once and Rufus felt, with a quailing of shame and fear, he sees me; but the man immediately looked away again and Rufus watched him until he was out of sight.

How would your daddy like it?

He thought of the way they teased him and did things to him, and how mad his father got when he just came home. He thought how different it would be today if he only didn't have to stay home from school.

He let himself out again and stole back between the houses to the alley, and walked along the alley, listening to the cinders cracking under each step, until he came near the sidewalk. He was not in front of his own home now, or even on Highland

Avenue; he was coming into the side street down from his home, and he felt that here nobody would identify him with his home and send him back to it. What he could see from the mouth of the alley was much less familiar to him, and he took the last few steps which brought him out onto the sidewalk with deliberation and shyness. He was doing something he had been told not to do.

He looked up the street and he could see the corner he knew so well, where he always met the others so unhappily, and, farther away, the corner around which his father always disappeared on the way to work, and first appeared on his way home from work. He felt it would be good luck that he would not be meeting them at that corner. Slowly, uneasily, he turned his head, and looked down the side street in the other direction; and there they were: three together, and two along the far side of the street, and one alone, farther off, and another alone, farther off, and, without importance to him, some girls here and there, as well. He knew the faces of all of these boys well, though he was not sure of any of their names. The moment he saw them all he was sure they saw him, and sure that they knew. He stood still and waited for them, looking from one to another of them, into their eyes, and step by step at their several distances, each of them at all times looking into his eyes and knowing, they came silently nearer. Waiting, in silence, during those many seconds before the first of them came really near him, he felt that it was so long to wait, and be watched so closely and silently, and to watch back, that he wanted to go back into the alley and not be seen by them or by anybody else, and yet at the same time he knew that they were all approaching him with the realization that something had happened to him that had not happened to any other boy in town, and that now at last they were bound to think well of him; and the nearer they came but were yet at a distance, the more the gray, sober air was charged with the great energy and with a sense of glory and of danger, and the deeper and more exciting the silence became, and the more tall, proud, shy and exposed he felt; so that as they came still nearer he once again felt his face break into a wide smile, with which he had nothing to do, and feeling that there was something deeply wrong in such a smile, tried his best to quieten his face and told them, shyly and proudly, "My daddy's dead."

Of the first three who came up, two merely looked at him and the third said, "Huh! Betcha he ain't"; and Rufus, astounded that they did not know and that they should disbelieve him, said, "Why he is so!"

"Where's your satchel at?" said the boy who had spoken. "You're just making up a lie so you can lay out of school."

"I am not laying out," Rufus replied. "I was going to school and my Aunt Hannah told me I didn't have to go to school today or tomorrow or not till—not for a few days. She said I mustn't. So I am not laying out. I'm just staying out."

And another of the boys said, "That's right. If his daddy is dead he don't have to go back to school till after the funerl."

While Rufus had been speaking two other boys had crossed over to join them and now one of them said, "He don't have to. He can lay out cause his daddy got killed," and Rufus looked at the boy gratefully and the boy looked back at him, it seemed to Rufus, with deference.

But the first boy who had spoken said, resentfully, "How do *you* know?"

And the second boy, while his companion nodded, said, "Cause my daddy seen it in the paper. Can't your daddy read the paper?"

The paper, Rufus thought; it's even in the paper! And he looked wisely at the first boy. And the first boy, interested enough to ignore the remark against his father, said, "Well how did he get killed, then?" and Rufus, realizing with respect that it was even more creditable to get killed than just to die, took a deep breath and said, "Why he was . . ."; but the boy whose father had seen it in the paper was already talking, so he listened, instead, feeling as if all this were being spoken for him, and on his behalf, and in his praise, and feeling it all the more as he looked from one silent boy to the next and saw that their eyes were constantly on him. And Rufus listened, too, with as much interest as they did, while the boy said with relish, "In his ole Tin Lizzie, that's how. He was driving along in his ole Tin Lizzie and it hit a rock and throwed him out in the ditch and run up a eight-foot bank and then fell back and turned over and over and landed right on top of him *whomph* and mashed every bone in his body, that's all. And somebody come and found him and he was dead already time they got there, that's how."

"He was instantly killed," Rufus began, and expected to go ahead and correct some of the details of the account, but nobody seemed to hear him, for two other boys had come up and just as he began to speak one of them said, "Your daddy got his name in the paper didn he, and you too," and he saw that now all the boys looked at him with new respect.

"He's dead," he told them. "He got killed."

"That's what my daddy says," one of them said, and the other said, "What you get for driving a auto when you're drunk, that's what my dad says," and the two of them looked gravely at the other boys, nodding, and at Rufus.

"What's drunk?" Rufus asked.

"What's drunk?" one of the boys mocked incredulously: "Drunk is fulla good ole whiskey"; and he began to stagger about in circles with his knees weak and his head lolling. "At's what drunk is."

"Then he wasn't," Rufus said.

"How do *you* know?"

"He wasn't drunk because that wasn't how he died. The wheel hit a rock and the other wheel, the one you steer with, just hit him on the chin, but it hit him so hard it killed him. He was instantly killed."

"What's instantly killed?" one of them asked.

"What do *you* care?" another said.

"Right off like that," an older boy explained, snapping his fingers. Another boy joined the group. Thinking of what instantly meant, and how his father's name was in the paper and his own too, and how he had got killed, not just died, he was not listening to them very clearly for a few moments, and then, all of a sudden, he began to realize that he was the center of everything and that they all knew it and that they waited to hear him tell the true account of it.

"I don't know nothing about no chin," the boy whose father saw it in the paper was saying. "Way I heard it he was a-drivin along in his ole Tin Lizzie and he hit a rock and ole Tin Lizzie run off the road and thowed him out and run up a eight-foot bank and turned over and over and fell back down on top of him *whomp*."

"How do *you* know?" an older boy was saying. "*You* wasn't there. Anybody here knows it's *him*." And he pointed at Rufus and Rufus was startled from his revery.

"Why?" asked the boy who had just come up.

"Cause it's his daddy," one of them explained.

"It's my daddy," Rufus said.

"What happened?" asked still another boy, at the fringe of the group.

"My daddy got killed," Rufus said.

"His daddy got killed," several of the others explained.

"My daddy says he bets he was drunk."

"Good ole whiskey!"

"Shut up, what's *your* daddy know about it."

"Was he drunk?"

"No," Rufus said.

"No," two others said.

"Let *him* tell it."

"Yeah, *you* tell it."

"Anybody here ought to know, it's him."

"Come on and tell us."

"Good ole whiskey."

"Shut your mouth."

"Well come on and tell us, then."

They became silent and all of them looked at him. Rufus looked back into their eyes in the sudden deep stillness. A man walked by, stepping into the gutter to skirt them.

Rufus said, quietly, "He was coming home from Grampa's last night, Grampa Follet. He's very sick and Daddy had to go up way in the middle of the night to see him, and he was hurrying as fast as he could to get back home because he was so late. And there was a cotter pin worked loose."

"What's a cotter pin?"

"Shut up."

"A cotter pin is what holds things together underneath, that you steer with. It worked loose and fell out so that when one of the front wheels hit a loose rock it wrenched the wheel and he couldn't steer and the auto ran down off the road with an awful bump and they saw where the wheel you steer with hit him right on the chin and he was instantly killed. He was thrown all the way out of the auto and it ran up an eight-foot emb—embackment and then it rolled back down and it was upside down beside him when they found him. There was not a mark on his body. Only a little tiny blue mark right on the end of the chin and another on his lip."

In the silence he could see the auto upside down with its wheels in the air and his father lying beside it with the little blue marks on his chin and on his lip.

"Heck," one of them said, "how can *that* kill anybody?"

He felt a kind of sullen stirring among the others, and he felt that he was not believed, or that they did not think very well of his father for being killed so easily.

"It was just exactly the way it just happened to hit him, Uncle Andrew says. He says it was just a chance in a million. It gave him a concush, con, concush—it did something to his brain that killed him."

"Just a chance in a million," one of the older boys said gravely, and another gravely nodded.

"A million trillion," another said.

"Knocked him crazy as a loon," another cried, and with a waggling forefinger he made a rapid blubbery noise against his loose lower lip.

"Shut yer Goddamn mouth," an older boy said coldly. "Ain't you got no sense at all?"

"Way I heard it, ole Tin Lizzie just rolled right back on top of him *whomp.*"

This account of it was false, Rufus was sure, but it seemed to him more exciting than his own, and more creditable to his father and to him, and nobody could question, scornfully, whether that could kill, as they could of just a blow on the chin; so he didn't try to contradict. He felt that he was lying, and in some way being disloyal as well, but he said only, "He was instantly killed. He didn't have to feel any pain."

"Never even knowed what hit him," a boy said quietly. "That's what my dad says."

"No," Rufus said. It had not occurred to him that way. "I guess he didn't." Never even knowed what hit him. Knew.

"Reckon that ole Tin Lizzie is done for now. Huh?"

He wondered if there was some meanness behind calling it an old Tin Lizzie. "I guess so," he said.

"Good old waggin, but she done broke down."

His father sang that.

"No more joy rides in that ole Tin Lizzie, huh, Rufus?"

"I guess not," Rufus replied shyly.

He began to realize that for some moments now a bell, the school bell, had been weltering on the dark gray air; he realized it because at this moment the last of its reverberations were fading.

"Last bell," one of the boys said in sudden alarm.

"Come on, we're goana git hell," another said; and within another second Rufus was watching them all run dwindling away up the street, and around the corner into Highland Avenue, as fast as they could go, and all round him the morning was empty and still. He stood still and watched the corner for almost half a minute after the fattest of them, and then the smallest, had disappeared; then he walked slowly back along the alley, hearing once more the sober crumbling of the cinders under each step, and up though the narrow side yard between the houses, and up the steps of the front porch.

In the paper! He looked for it beside the door, but it was not there. He listened carefully, but he could not hear anything. He let himself quietly through the front door, at the moment his Aunt Hannah came from the sitting room into the front hall. She wore a cloth over her hair and in her hands she was carrying the smoking stand. She did not see him at first and he saw how fierce and lonely her face looked. He tried to make himself small but just then she wheeled on him, her lenses flashing, and exclaimed, "Rufus Follet, where on earth have you been!" His stomach quailed, for her voice was so angry it was as if it were crackling with sparks.

"Outdoors."

"Where, outdoors! I've been looking for you all over the place."

"Just out. Back in the alley."

"Didn't you hear me calling you?"

He shook his head.

"I shouted until my voice was hoarse."

He kept shaking his head. "Honest," he said.

"Now listen to me carefully. You mustn't go outdoors today. Stay right here inside this house, do you understand?"

He nodded. He felt suddenly that he had done an awful thing.

"I know it's hard to," she said more gently, "but you've got to. Help Catherine with her coloring. Read a book. You promise?"

"Yes'm."

"And don't do anything to disturb your mother."

"No'm."

She went on down the hall and he watched her. What was she doing with the pipes and the ashtrays, he wondered. He considered sneaking behind her, for he knew that she could not see at all well, yet he would be sure to get caught, for her hearing was very sharp. All the same, he sneaked along to the back of the hall and watched her empty the ashes into the garbage pail and rap out the pipes against its rim. Then she stood with the pipes in her hand, looking around uncertainly; finally she put the pipes and the ashtrays on the cupboard shelf, and set the smoking stand in the corner of the kitchen behind the stove. He went back along the hall on tiptoe and into the sitting room.

Catherine sat in the little chair by the side window with a picture book on her knees. Her crayons were all over the window sill and she was working intently with an orange crayon. She looked up when he came in and looked down again and kept on working.

He did not want to help her, he wanted to be by himself and see if he could find the paper with the names in it, but he felt that he ought to try to be good, for by now he felt a dark uneasiness about something, he was not quite sure what, that he had done. He walked over to her. "I'll help you," he said.

"No," Catherine said, without even looking up. It was the Mother Goose book and with her orange crayon she was scrawling all over the cow which jumped over the moon, inside and outside the lines of the cow.

"Aunt Hannah says to," he said, disgusted to see what she was doing to the cow.

"No," Catherine said, and again she did not look up or stop scrawling for a second.

"That ain't no color for a cow," he said. "Whoever saw an orange cow?" She made no reply, but he could see that her face was getting red. "Besides, you're not even coloring inside the cow," he said. "Just look at that. You're just running that crayon around all over the place and it isn't even the right color." She bore down even harder and harder with the crayon and pushed it in a wider and wider tangle of lines and all of a sudden it snapped and the long part rolled to the floor. "See now, you busted it," Rufus said.

"Leave me alone!" She tried to draw with the stub of the crayon but it was too short, and the paper got in the way. She looked along the window sill and selected a brown crayon.

"What you gonna do with that brown one?" Rufus said. "You already got all that orange all over everything, what you gonna do with that brown one?" Catherine took the brown crayon and made a brutal tangle of dark lines all over the orange lines. "Now all you did is just spoil it," Rufus said. "You don't know how to draw!"

"*Quit* it!" Catherine yelled, and all of a sudden she was crying. He heard his Aunt Hannah's sharp voice from the kitchen: "Rufus?"

He was furious with Catherine. "Crybaby," he whispered with cold hatred: "Tattletale!"

And there was Aunt Hannah at the door, just as mad as a hornet. "Now, what's the matter? What have you done to her?" She walked straight at him.

It wasn't fair. How did she know he was doing anything? With a feeling of real righteousness he talked back: "I didn't do one single thing to her. She was just messing everything up on her picture and I tried to help her like you told me to and all of a sudden she started to cry."

"What did he do, Catherine?"

"He wouldn't let me alone."

"Why good night, I never even touched you and you're a liar if you say I did!"

All of a sudden he felt himself gripped by the shoulders and shaken and he turned his rattling head from his sister to look into his Aunt Hannah's freezing glare.

"Now you just listen to me," she said. "Are you listening?" she sputtered. *"Are you listening?"* she said still more intensely.

"Yes," he managed to get out, though the word was all shaken up.

"I don't want to spank you on this day of all days, but if I hear you say one more rough thing like that to your sister I'll give you a spanking you'll remember to your dying day, do you hear me? *Do you hear me?*"

"Yes."

"And if you tease her or make her cry just one more time I'll—I'll turn the whole matter over to your Uncle Andrew and we'll see what *he'll* do about it. Do you want me to call him? He's upstairs this minute! Shall I call him?'' She stopped shaking him and looked at him. ''Shall I?'' He shook his head; he was terrified. ''All right, but this is my last warning. Do you understand?''

''Yes'm.''

''Now if you can't play with Catherine in peace like a decent boy just—stay by yourself. Look at some pictures. Read a book. But you be quiet. And good. Do you hear me?''

''Yes'm.''

''Very well.'' She stood up and her joints snapped. ''Come with me, Catherine,'' she said. ''Let's bring your crayons.'' And she helped Catherine gather up the crayons and the stubs from the window sill and from the carpet. Catherine's face was still red but she was not crying any more. As she passed Rufus she gave him a glance filled with satisfaction, and he answered it with a glance of helpless malevolence.

He listened towards upstairs. If his Uncle Andrew had overheard this, there would really be trouble. But there was no evidence that he had. Rufus felt weak in the knees and in the stomach. He went over to the chair beside the fireplace and sat down.

It was mean to pester Catherine like that but he hadn't wanted to do anything for her anyway. And why did she have to holler like that and bring Aunt Hannah running? He remembered the way her face got red and he knew that he had really been mean to her and he was sorry. But what did she holler for, like a regular crybaby? He would be very careful today, but sooner or later he sure would get back on her. Darn crybaby. Tattletale.

The others really did pay him some attention, though. Anybody here ought to know, it's him. His daddy got killed. Yeah *you* tell it. Come on and tell us. Just a chance in a million. A million trillion. Never even knowed, knew, what hit him. Shut yer Goddamn mouth. Ain't you got no sense at all?

Instantly killed.

Concussion, that was it. Concussion of the brain.

Knocked him crazy as a loon, bibblibblebble.

Shut yer Goddamn mouth.

But there was something that made him feel wrong.

Ole Tin Lizzie.

What you get for driving a auto when you're drunk, that's what my dad says.

Good ole whiskey.

Something he did.

Ole Tin Lizzie just rolled back down on top of him *whomp*.

Didn't either.

He didn't say it didn't. Not clear enough.

Heck, how can that kill anybody?

Did, though. Just a chance in a million. Million trillion.

Instantly killed.

Worse than that, he did.

What.

How would your daddy like it?

He would like me to be with them without them teasing; looking up to me.

How would your daddy like it?

Like what?

Going out in the street like that when he is dead.

Out in the street like what?

Showing off to people because he is dead.

He wants me to get along with them.

So I tell them he is dead and they look up to me, they don't tease me.

Showing off because he's dead, that's all you can show off about. Any other thing they'd tease me and I wouldn't fight back.

How would your daddy like it?

But he likes me to get along with them. That's why I—went out—showed off.

He felt so uneasy, deep inside his stomach, that he could not think about it any more. He wished he hadn't done it. He wished he could go back and not do anything of the kind. He wished his father could know about it and tell him that yes he was bad but it was all right he didn't mean to be bad. He was glad his father didn't know because if his father knew he would think even worse of him than ever. But if his father's soul was around, always, watching over them, then he knew. And that was worst of anything because there was no way to hide from a soul, and no way to talk to it, either. He just knows, and it couldn't say anything to him, and he couldn't say anything to it. It couldn't whip him either, but it could sit and look at him and be ashamed of him.

"I didn't mean it," he said aloud. "I didn't mean to do bad."

I wanted to show you my cap, he added, silently.

He looked at his father's morsechair.

Not a mark on his body.

He still looked at the chair. With a sense of deep stealth and secrecy he finally went over and stood beside it. After a few moments, and after listening most intently, to be sure that nobody was near, he smelled of the chair, its deeply hollowed seat, the arms, the back. There was only a cold smell of tobacco and, high along the back, a faint smell of hair. He thought of the ashtray on its weighted strap on the arm; it was empty. He ran his finger inside it; there was only a dim smudge of ash. There was nothing like enough to keep in his pocket or wrap up in a paper. He looked at his finger for a moment and licked it; his tongue tasted of darkness.

THE ROCKING-HORSE WINNER

THERE WAS A WOMAN who was beautiful, who started with all the advantages, yet she had no luck. She married for love, and the love turned to dust. She had bonny children, yet she felt they had been thrust upon her, and she could not love them. They looked at her coldly, as if they were finding fault with her. And hurriedly she felt she must cover up some fault in herself. Yet what it was that she must cover up she never knew. Nevertheless, when her children were present, she always felt the centre of her heart go hard. This troubled her, and in her manner she was all the more gentle and anxious for her children, as if she loved them very much. Only she herself knew that at the centre of her heart was a hard little place that could not feel love, no, not for anybody. Everybody else said of her: "She is such a good mother. She adores her children." Only she herself, and her children themselves, knew that it was not so. They read it in each other's eyes.

There were a boy and two little girls. They lived in a pleasant house, with a garden, and they had discreet servants, and felt themselves superior to anyone in the neighbourhood.

Although they lived in style, they felt always an anxiety in the house. There was never enough money. The mother had a small income, and the father had a small income, but not nearly enough for the social position which they had to keep up. The father went into town to some office. But though he had good prospects, these prospects never materialized. There was always the grinding sense of the shortage of money, though the style was always kept up.

At last the mother said: "I will see if I can't make something." But she did not know where to begin. She racked her brains, and tried this thing and the other, but could not find anything successful. The failure made deep lines come into her face. Her children were growing up, they would have to go to school. There must be more money, there must be more money. The father, who was always very handsome and expensive in his tastes, seemed as if he never would be able to do anything worth doing. And the mother, who had a great belief in herself, did not succeed any better, and her tastes were just as expensive.

And so the house came to be haunted by the unspoken phrase: There must be more money! There must be more money! The children could hear it all the time, though nobody said it aloud. They heard it at Christmas, when the expensive and splendid toys filled the nursery. Behind the shining modern rocking-horse, behind the smart doll's house, a voice would start whispering: "There must be more money! There must be more money!" And the children would stop playing, to listen for a moment. They would look into each other's eyes, to see if they had all heard. And each one saw in the eyes of the other two that they too had heard. "There must be more money! There must be more money!"

It came whispering from the springs of the still-swaying rocking-horse, and even the horse, bending his wooden, champing head, heard it. The big doll, sitting so pink and smirking in her new pram, could hear it quite plainly, and seemed to be smirking all the more self-consciously because of it. The foolish puppy, too, that took the place of the teddy-bear, he was looking so extraordinarily foolish for no other reason but that he heard the secret whisper all over the house: "There must be more money!"

Yet nobody ever said it aloud. The whisper was everywhere, and therefore no one spoke it. Just as no one ever says: "We are breathing!" in spite of the fact that breath is coming and going all the time.

"Mother," said the boy Paul one day, "why don't we keep a car of our own? Why do we always use uncle's, or else a taxi?"

"Because we're the poor members of the family," said the mother.

"But why are we, mother?"

"Well—I suppose," she said slowly and bitterly, "it's because your father has no luck."

The boy was silent for some time.

"Is luck money, mother?" he asked, rather timidly.

"No, Paul. Not quite. It's what causes you to have money."

"Oh!" said Paul vaguely. "I thought when Uncle Oscar said filthy lucker, it meant money."

"Filthy lucre does mean money," said the mother. "But it's lucre, not luck."

"Oh!" said the boy. "Then what is luck, mother?"

"It's what causes you to have money. If you're lucky you have money. That's why it's better to be born lucky than rich. If you're rich, you may lose your money. But if you're lucky, you will always get more money."

"Oh! Will you? And is father not lucky?"

"Very unlucky, I should say," she said bitterly.

The boy watched her with unsure eyes.

"Why?" he asked.

"I don't know. Nobody ever knows why one person is lucky and another unlucky."

"Don't they? Nobody at all? Does nobody know?"

"Perhaps God. But He never tells."

"He ought to, then. And aren't you lucky either, mother?"

"I can't be, if I married an unlucky husband."

"But by yourself, aren't you?"

"I used to think I was, before I married. Now I think I

am very unlucky indeed.''

"Why?''

"Well—never mind! Perhaps I'm not really,'' she said.

The child looked at her, to see if she meant it. But he saw, by the lines of her mouth, that she was only trying to hide something from him.

"Well anyhow,'' he said stoutly, "I'm a lucky person.''

"Why?'' said his mother, with a sudden laugh.

He stared at her. He didn't even know why he had said it.

"God told me,'' he asserted, brazening it out.

"I hope He did, dear!'' she said, again with a laugh, but rather bitter.

"He did, mother!''

"Excellent!'' said the mother, using one of her husband's exclamations.

The boy saw she did not believe him; or, rather, that she paid no attention to his assertion. This angered him somewhat, and made him want to compel her attention.

He went off by himself, vaguely, in a childish way, seeking for the clue to "luck." Absorbed, taking no heed of other people, he went about with a sort of stealth, seeking inwardly for luck. He wanted luck, he wanted it, he wanted it. When the two girls were playing dolls in the nursery, he would sit on his big rocking-horse, charging madly into space, with a frenzy that made the little girls peer at him uneasily. Wildly the horse careered, the waving dark hair of the boy tossed, his eyes had a strange glare in them. The little girls dared not to speak to him.

When he had ridden to the end of his mad little journey, he climbed down and stood in front of his rocking-horse, staring fixedly into its lowered face. Its red mouth was slightly open, its big eye was wide and glassy-bright.

"Now!'' he would silently command the snorting steed.

"Now, take me to where there is luck! Now take me!"

And he would slash the horse on the neck with the little whip he had asked Uncle Oscar for. He knew the horse could take him to where there was luck, if only he forced it. So he would mount again, and start on his furious ride, hoping at last to get there. He knew he could get there.

"You'll break your horse, Paul!" said the nurse.

"He's always riding like that! I wish he'd leave off!" said his elder sister Joan.

But he only glared down on them in silence. Nurse gave him up. She could make nothing of him. Anyhow he was growing beyond her.

One day his mother and his Uncle Oscar came in when he was on one of his furious rides. He did not speak to them.

"Hallo, you young jockey! Riding a winner?" said his uncle.

"Aren't you growing too big for a rocking-horse? You're not a very little boy any longer, you know," said his mother.

But Paul only gave a blue glare from his big, rather close-set eyes. He would speak to nobody when he was in full tilt. His mother watched him with an anxious expression on her face.

At last he suddenly stopped forcing his horse into the mechanical gallop, and slid down.

"Well, I got there!" he announced fiercely, his blue eyes still flaring, and his sturdy long legs straddling apart.

"Where did you get to?" asked his mother.

"Where I wanted to go," he flared back at her.

"That's right, son!" said Uncle Oscar. "Don't you stop till you get there. What's the horse's name?"

"He doesn't have a name," said the boy.

"Gets on without all right?" asked the uncle.

"Well, he has different names. He was called Sansovino last

week.''

"Sansovino, eh? Won the Ascot. How did you know his name?''

"He always talks about horse-races with Bassett,'' said Joan.

The uncle was delighted to find that his small nephew was posted with all the racing news. Bassett, the young gardener, who had been wounded in the left foot in the war and had got his present job through Oscar Cresswell, whose batman he had been, was a perfect blade of the "turf.'' He lived in the racing events, and the small boy lived with him.

Oscar Cresswell got it all from Bassett.

"Master Paul comes and asks me, so I can't do more than tell him, sir,'' said Bassett, his face terribly serious, as if he were speaking of religious matters.

"And does he ever put anything on a horse he fancies?''

"Well—I don't want to give him away—he's a young sport, a fine sport, sir. Would you mind asking him yourself? He sort of takes a pleasure in it, and perhaps he'd feel I was giving him away, sir, if you don't mind.''

Bassett was serious as a church.

The uncle went back to his nephew, and took him off for a ride in the car.

"Say, Paul, old man, do you ever put anything on a horse?'' the uncle asked.

The boy watched the handsome man closely.

"Why, do you think I oughtn't to?'' he parried.

"Not a bit of it! I thought perhaps you might give me a tip for the Lincoln.''

The car sped on into the country, going down to Uncle Ocsar's place in Hampshire.

"Honour bright?'' said the nephew.

"Honour bright, son!'' said the uncle.

"Well, then, Daffodil."

"Daffodil! I doubt it, sonny. What about Mirza?"

"I only know the winner," said the boy. "That's Daffodil"

"Daffodil, eh?"

There was a pause. Daffodil was an obscure horse comparatively.

"Uncle!"

"Yes, son?"

"You won't let it go any further, will you? I promised Bassett."

"Bassett be damned, old man! What's he got to do with it?"

"We're partners. We've been partners from the first. Uncle, he lent me my first five shillings, which I lost. I promised him, honour bright, it was only between me and him; only you gave me that ten-shilling note I started winning with, so I thought you were lucky. You won't let it go any further, will you?"

The boy gazed at his uncle from those big, hot, blue eyes, set rather close together. The uncle stirred and laughed uneasily.

"Right you are, son! I'll keep your tip private. Daffodil, eh? How much are you putting on him?"

"All except twenty pounds," said the boy. "I keep that in reserve."

The uncle thought it a good joke.

"You keep twenty pounds in reserve, do you, you young romancer? What are you betting then?"

"I'm betting three hundred," said the boy gravely. "But it's between you and me, Uncle Oscar! Honour bright?"

The uncle burst into a roar of laughter.

"It's between you and me all right, you young Nat Gould," he said, laughing. "But where's your three hundred?"

"Bassett keeps it for me. We're partners."

"You are, are you? And what is Bassett putting on Daffodil?"

"He won't go quite as high as I do, I expect. Perhaps he'll go a hundred and fifty."

"What, pennies?" laughed the uncle.

"Pounds," said the child, with a surprised look at his uncle. "Bassett keeps a bigger reserve than I do."

Between wonder and amusement Uncle Oscar was silent. He pursued the matter no further, but he determined to take his nephew with him to the Lincoln races.

"Now, son," he said, "I'm putting twenty on Mirza, and I'll put five for you on any horse you fancy. What's your pick?"

"Daffodil, uncle."

"No, not the fiver on Daffodil!"

"I should if it was my own fiver," said the child.

"Good! Good! Right you are! A fiver for me and a fiver for you on Daffodil."

The child had never been to a race-meeting before, and his eyes were blue fire. He pursed his mouth tight, and watched. A Frenchman just in front had put his money on Lancelot. Wild with excitement, he flayed his arms up and down, yelling "Lancelot! Lancelot!" in his French accent.

Daffodil came in first, Lancelot second, Mirza third. The child, flushed and with eyes blazing, was curiously serene. His uncle brought him four five-pound notes, four to one.

"What am I to do with these?" he cried, waving them before the boy's eyes.

"I suppose we'll talk to Bassett," said the boy. "I expect I have fifteen hundred now; and twenty in reserve; and this twenty."

His uncle studied him for some moments.

"Look here, son!" he said. "You're not serious about

Bassett and that fifteen hundred, are you?"

"Yes, I am. But it's between you and me, uncle. Honour bright!"

"Honour bright all right, son! But I must talk to Bassett."

"If you'd like to be a partner, uncle, with Bassett and me, we could all be partners. Only, you'd have to promise, honour bright, uncle, not to let it go beyond us three. Bassett and I are lucky, and you must be lucky, because it was your ten shillings I started winning with..."

Uncle Oscar took both Bassett and Paul into Richmond Park for an afternoon, and there they talked.

"It's like this, you see, sir," Bassett said. "Master Paul would get me talking about racing events, spinning yarns, you know, sir. And he was always keen on knowing if I'd made or if I'd lost. It's about a year since, now, that I put five shillings on Blush of Dawn for him—and we lost. Then the luck turned, with that ten shillings he had from you, that we put on Singhalese. And since that time, it's been pretty steady, all things considering. What do you say, Master Paul?"

"We're all right when we're sure," said Paul. "It's when we're not quite sure that we go down."

"Oh, but we're careful then," said Bassett.

"But when are you sure?" smiled Uncle Oscar.

"It's Master Paul, sir," said Bassett, in a secret, religious voice. "It's as if he had it from heaven. Like Daffodil, now, for the Lincoln. That was as sure as eggs."

"Did you put anything on Daffodil?" asked Oscar Cresswell.

"Yes, sir. I made my bit."

"And my nephew?"

Bassett was obstinately silent, looking at Paul.

"I made twelve hundred, didn't I, Bassett? I told uncle I was putting three hundred on Daffodil."

"That's right," said Bassett, nodding.

"But where's the money?" asked the uncle.

"I keep it safe locked up, sir. Master Paul he can have it any minute he likes to ask for it."

"What, fifteen hundred pounds?"

"And twenty! And forty, that is, with the twenty he made on the course."

"It's amazing!" said the uncle.

"If Master Paul offers you to be partners, sir, I would, if I were you; if you'll excuse me," said Bassett.

Oscar Cresswell thought about it.

"I'll see the money," he said.

They drove home again, and sure enough, Bassett came round to the garden-house with fifteen hundred pounds in notes. The twenty pounds reserve was left with Joe Glee, in the Turf Commission deposit.

"You see, it's all right, uncle, when I'm sure! Then we go strong, for all we're worth. Don't we, Bassett?"

"We do that, Master Paul."

"And when are you sure?" said the uncle, laughing.

"Oh, well, sometimes I'm absolutely sure, like about Daffodil," said the boy; "and sometimes I have an idea; and sometimes I haven't even an idea, have I Bassett? Then we're careful, because we mostly go down.

"You do, do you! And when you're sure, like about Daffodil, what makes you sure, sonny?"

"Oh, well, I don't know," said the boy uneasily. "I'm sure, you know, uncle; that's all."

"It's as if he had it from heaven, sir," Bassett reiterated.

"I should say so!" said the uncle.

But he became a partner. And when the Leger was coming on, Paul was "sure" about Lively Spark, which was a quite inconsiderable horse. The boy insisted on putting a thousand on the horse, Basset went for five hundred, and Oscar Cresswell two hundred. Lively Spark came in first, and the betting had been ten to one against him. Paul had made ten thousand.

"You see," he said. "I was absolutely sure of him."

Even Oscar Cresswell had cleared two thousand.

"Look here, son," he said, "this sort of thing makes me nervous."

"It needn't uncle! Perhaps I shan't be sure again for a long time."

"But what are you going to do with your money?" asked the uncle.

"Of course," said the boy, "I started it for mother. She said she had no luck, because father is unlucky, so I thought if I was lucky, it might stop whispering."

"What might stop whispering?"

"Our house. I hate our house for whispering."

"What does it whisper?"

"Why—Why"—the boy fidgeted—"why, I don't know. But it's always short of money, you know, uncle."

"I know it, son, I know it."

"You know people send mother writs, don't you uncle?"

"I'm afraid I do," said the uncle.

"And then the house whispers, like people laughing at you behind your back. It's awful, that is! I thought if I was lucky . . ."

"You might stop it," added the uncle.

The boy watched him with big blue eyes that had an uncanny cold fire in them, and he said never a word.

"Well, then!" said the uncle. "What are we doing?"

"I shouldn't like mother to know I was lucky," said the boy.

"Why not, son?"

"She'd stop me."

"I don't think she would."

"Oh!"—and the boy writhed in an odd way—"I don't want her to know, uncle."

"All right, son! We'll manage it without her knowing."

They managed it very easily. Paul, at the other's suggestion, handed over five thousand pounds to his uncle, who deposited it with the family lawyer, who was then to inform Paul's mother that a relative had put five thousand pounds into his hands, which sum was to be paid out a thousand pounds at a time, on the mother's birthday, for the next five years.

"So she'll have a birthday present of a thousand pounds for five successive years," said Uncle Oscar. "I hope it won't make it all the harder for her later."

Paul's mother had her birthday in November. The house had been "whispering" worse than ever lately, and, even in spite of his luck, Paul could not bear up against it. He was very anxious to see the effect of the birthday letter, telling his mother about the thousand pounds.

When there were no visitors, Paul now took his meals with his parents, as he was beyond the nursery control. His mother went into town nearly every day. She had discovered that she had an odd knack of sketching furs and dress materials, so she worked secretly in the studio of a friend who was the chief "artist" for the leading drapers. She drew the figures of ladies in furs and ladies in silk and sequins for the newspaper advertisements. This young woman artist earned several thousand pounds a year, but Paul's mother only made several hundreds, and she was again dissatisfied. She so wanted to be the first in something, and she did not succeed, even in making sketches for drapery advertisements.

She was down to breakfast on the morning of her birthday. Paul watched her face as she read her letters. He knew the lawyer's letter. As his mother read it, her face hardened and became more expressionless. Then a cold, determined look came on her mouth. She hid the letter under the pile of others, and said not a word about it.

"Didn't you have anything nice in the post for your birthday, mother?" said Paul.

"Quite moderately nice," she said, her voice cold and absent.

She went away to town without saying more.

But in the afternoon Uncle Oscar appeared. He said Paul's mother had had a long interview with the lawyer, asking if the whole five thousand could be advanced at once, as she was in debt.

"What do you think, uncle?" said the boy.

"I leave it to you, son."

"Oh, let her have it, then! We can get some more with the other," said the boy.

"A bird in the hand is worth two in the bush, laddie!"

"But I'm sure to know for the Grand National; or the Lincolnshire; or else the Derby. I'm sure to know for one of them," said Paul.

So Uncle Oscar signed the agreement, and Paul's mother touched the whole five thousand. Then something very curious happened. The voices in the house suddenly went mad, like a chorus of frogs on a spring evening. There were certain new furnishings, and Paul had a tutor. He was really going to Eton, his father's school, in the following autumn. There were flowers in the winter, and a blossoming of the luxury Paul's mother had been used to. And yet the voices in the house, behind the sprays of mimosa and almond blossom, and from under the piles of iridescent cushions, simply trilled and screamed in a sort of ecstasy: "There must be more money! Oh-h-h, there must be more money. Oh, now, now-w!

Now-w-w—there must be more money!—more than ever!
More than ever!''

It frightened Paul terribly. He studied away at his Latin and
Greek with his tutors. But his intense hours were spent with
Bassett. The Grand National had gone by: he had not
"known," and had lost a hundred pounds. Summer was at
hand. He was in agony for the Lincoln. But even for the
Lincoln he didn't "know" and he lost fifty pounds. He
became wild-eyed and strange, as if something were going
to explode in him.

"Let it alone, son! Don't you bother about it!" urged Uncle
Oscar. But it was as if the boy couldn't really hear what his
uncle was saying.

"I've got to know for the Derby! I've got to know for the
Derby!" the child reiterated, his big blue eyes blazing with a
sort of madness.

His mother noticed how overwrought he was.

"You'd better go to the seaside. Wouldn't you like to go
now to the seaside, instead of waiting? I think you'd better,"
she said, looking down at him anxiously, her heart curiously
heavy because of him.

But the child lifted his uncanny blue eyes.

"I couldn't possibly go before the Derby, mother!" he said.
"I couldn't possibly!"

"Why not?" she said, her voice becoming heavy when she
was opposed. "Why not? You can still go from the seaside to
see the Derby with your Uncle Oscar, if that's what you wish.
No need for you to wait here. Besides, I think you care too
much about these races. It's a bad sign. My family has been a
gambling family, and you won't know till you grow up how
much damage it has done. But it has done damage. I shall have
to send Bassett away, and ask Uncle Oscar not to talk racing
to you, unless you promise to be reasonable about it; go away

to the seaside and forget it. You're all nerves!''

"I'll do what you like, mother, so long as you don't send me away till after the Derby," the boy said.

"Send you away from where? Just from this house?"

"Yes," he said, gazing at her.

"Why, you curious child, what makes you care about this house so much, suddenly? I never knew you loved it."

He gazed at her without speaking. He had a secret within a secret, something he had not divulged, even to Bassett or to his Uncle Oscar.

But his mother, after standing undecided and a little bit sullen for some moments, said:

"Very well, then! Don't go to the seaside till after the Derby, if you don't wish it. But promise me you won't let your nerves go to pieces. Promise you won't think so much about horse-racing and events, as you call them!"

"Oh, no," said the boy casually. "I won't think much about them, mother. You needn't worry. I wouldn't worry, mother, if I were you."

"If you were me and I were you," said his mother, "I wonder what we should do!"

"But you know you needn't worry, mother, don't you?" the boy repeated.

"I should be awfully glad to know it," she said wearily.

"Oh, well, you can, you know. I mean, you ought to know you needn't worry," he insisted.

"Ought I? Then I'll see about it," she said.

Paul's secret of secrets was his wooden horse, that which had no name. Since he was emancipated from a nurse and a nursery-governess, he had had his rocking-horse removed to his own bedroom at the top of the house.

"Surely, you're too big for a rocking-horse!" his mother had remonstrated.

"Well, you see, mother, till I can have a real horse, I like to have some sort of animal about," had been his quaint answer.

"Do you feel he keeps you company?" she laughed.

"Oh, yes! He's very good, he always keeps me company, when I'm there," said Paul.

So the horse, rather shabby, stood in an arrested prance in the boy's bedroom.

The Derby was drawing near, and the boy grew more and more tense. He hardly heard what was spoken to him, he was very frail, and his eyes were really uncanny. His mother had sudden seizures of uneasiness about him. Sometimes, for half-an-hour, she would feel a sudden anxiety about him that was almost anguish. She wanted to rush to him at once, and know he was safe.

Two nights before the Derby, she was at a big party in town, when one of her rushes of anxiety about her boy, her firstborn, gripped her heart till she could hardly speak. She fought with the feeling, might and main, for she believed in common sense. But it was too strong. She had to leave the dance and go downstairs to telephone to the country. The children's nursery-governess was terribly surprised and startled at being rung up in the night.

"Are the children all right, Miss Wilmot?"

"Oh, yes, they are quite all right."

"Master Paul? Is he all right?"

"He went to bed as right as a trivet. Shall I run up and look at him?"

"No," said Paul's mother reluctantly. "No! Don't trouble. It's all right. Don't sit up. We shall be home fairly soon." She did not want her son's privacy intruded upon.

"Very good," said the governess.

It was about one o'clock when Paul's mother and father drove up to their house. All was still. Paul's mother went to her room and slipped off her white fur coat. She had told her maid not to wait up for her. She heard her husband downstairs, mixing a whisky-and-soda.

And then, because of the strange anxiety at her heart, she stole upstairs to her son's room. Noiselessly she went along the upper corridor. Was there a faint noise. What was it?

She stood, with arrested muscles, outside his door, listening. There was a strange, heavy, and yet not loud noise. Her heart stood still. It was a soundless noise, yet rushing and powerful. Something huge, in violent, hushed motion. What was it? What in God's name was it? She ought to know. She felt that she knew the noise. She knew what it was.

Yet she could not place it. She couldn't say what it was. And on and on it went, like a madness.

Softly, frozen with anxiety and fear, she turned the doorhandle.

The room was dark. Yet in the space near the window, she heard and saw something plunging to and fro. She gazed in fear and amazement.

Then suddenly she switched on the light, and saw her son, in his green pyjamas, madly surging on the rocking-horse. The blaze of light suddenly lit him up, as he urged the wooden horse, and lit her up, as she stood, blonde, in her dress of pale green and crystal, in the doorway.

"Paul!" she cried. "Whatever are you doing?"

"It's Malabar!" he screamed, in a powerful, strange voice. "It's Malabar."

His eyes blazed at her for one strange and senseless second, as he ceased urging his wooden horse. Then he fell with a crash to the ground, and she, all her tormented motherhood flooding upon her, rushed to gather him up.

But he was unconscious, and unconscious he remained, with some brain-fever. He talked and tossed, and his mother sat stonily by his side.

"Malabar! It's Malabar! Bassett, Bassett, I know! It's Malabar!"

So the child cried, trying to get up and urge the rocking-horse that gave him his inspiration.

"What does he mean by Malabar?" asked the heart-frozen mother.

"I don't know," said the father stonily.

"What does he mean by Malabar?" she asked her brother Oscar.

"It's one of the horses running for the Derby," was the answer.

And, in spite of himself, Oscar Cresswell spoke to Bassett, and himself put a thousand on Malabar: at fourteen to one.

The third day of the illness was critical: they were waiting for a change. The boy, with his rather long, curly hair, was tossing ceaselessly on the pillow. He neither slept nor regained consciousness, and his eyes were like blue stones. His mother sat, feeling her heart had gone, turned actually into a stone.

In the evening, Oscar Cresswell did not come, but Bassett sent a message, saying could he come up for one moment, just one moment? Paul's mother was very angry at the intrusion, but on second thought she agreed. The boy was the same. Perhaps Bassett might bring him to consciousness.

The gardener, a shortish fellow with a little brown moustache, and sharp little brown eyes, tiptoed into the room, touched his imaginary cap to Paul's mother, and stole to the bedside, staring with glittering, smallish eyes, at the tossing, dying child.

"Master Paul!" he whispered. "Master Paul! Malabar come in first all right, a clean win. I did as you told me. You've made over seventy thousand pounds, you have; you've got over eighty thousand. Malabar came in all right, Master Paul!''

"Malabar! Malabar! Did I say Malabar, mother? Did I say Malabar? Do you think I'm lucky, mother? I knew Malabar, didn't I? Over eighty thousand pounds! I call that lucky, don't you, mother? Over eighty thousand pounds! I knew, didn't I know I knew? Malabar came in all right. If I ride my horse till I'm sure, then I tell you, Bassett, you can go as high as you like. Did you go for all you were worth, Bassett?''

"I went a thousand on it, Master Paul."

"I never told you, mother, that if I can ride my horse, and get there, then I'm absolutely sure—oh, absolutely! Mother, did I ever tell you? I am lucky."

"No, you never did," said the mother.

But the boy died in the night.

And even as he lay dead, his mother heard her brother's voice saying to her: "My God, Hester, you're eighty-odd thousand to the good and a poor devil of a son to the bad. But, poor devil, poor devil, he's best gone out of a life where he rides his rocking-horse to find a winner.''

THE ZODIACS

WHEN I WAS in the seventh grade at P.S. 92 in Brooklyn, Louie Hirshfield was the only one of my friends who wasn't a good ballplayer. Which is putting it mildly. Louie was probably the worst athlete in the history of our school. He was also the smartest kid in our class and you'd think this combination would have made him the most unpopular guy in the world. It didn't. He wasn't especially well liked, but nobody resented him. Maybe it was because he let you copy from his homework—or maybe it was just because he didn't put on any airs about being so smart. In fact, Louie didn't put on airs about anything. He was one of the quietest kids I've ever met.

The only time I ever saw him excited—outside of what happened with him and our baseball team—was when our fathers would take the two of us to baseball games at Ebbets Field. Louie lived one floor under me, in my apartment building on Lenox Road, and we had grown up together, so I knew lots about Louie that nobody in school knew. He was an interesting guy, with lots of hobbies—tropical fish, rocks, stamps, Chinese puzzles, magic tricks, autographs.

That was the one thing the guys in school did know about. I don't know how many days he'd waited outside of Ebbets Field to get them, all I know is he had the best collection of baseball players' signatures of any guy in school. Lots of them were addressed personally, to—like, "To Louie, with best wishes from Jackie Robinson." What amazed me most about Louie, though, was that he could figure out a player's batting average in his head! If a guy got a hit his first time up in a game, Louie would say, "That raises his average to .326—" or whatever it was, and sure enough, the next time the guy came up, when the announcer would give the average, Louie would be right.

Louie had no illusions about his athletic ability either; he was never one of those guys who hang around when you're choosing up sides for a punchball or stickball game so that you *have* to pick him. And whenever he did play—like in gym class at school—he did what you told him and tried to stay out of the way.

That was why I was so surprised when he came up to my house one night after supper and asked if he could be on my baseball team.

"Gee Louie," I said, "we got more than nine guys already—anyway we're not even an official team or anything. We'll be lucky if we get to play more than five or six games all year."

"I don't really want to play," said Louie. "I—I just want to be on your team—"

"Well, I suppose you can come to practices and games," I said, "but I can't promise you'll ever get in a game."

"Honest, Howie—I know all the guys on your team are better than me. I wasn't even thinking of playing. What I'd like to do is be your general manager—"

His eyes really lit up when he said that. I looked at him, puzzled.

"Look," he said. "What do you think makes the Dodgers draw almost as many fans as the Yankees—? What was it that made people stick with the Dodgers when they were hardly in the league?"

"I don't know," I said. "They were just Dodger fans, I guess."

"Sure—that's it. Don't you see? Being a Dodger fan means something because being a Dodger means something colorful to the fans. And you know why? Because the Dodgers have

what my dad calls 'a good press'—they know how to get head-
lines in the papers whether they're winning or losing.''

"I guess so," I said. "But what's that got to do with us?"

"What's your team like now—? I'll tell you. It's the same
as ten thousand other teams of guys our age all over Brooklyn.
Nobody cares if you win or lose—except maybe you guys. If
I'm general manager, Howie, I'll promise you this—your
team will be noticed. Guys won't say 'we got a game with
Howie's team'—they won't come to the Parade Grounds to
see all the older guys play. They'll come to see the *Zodiacs—!*''

"The who—?"

Louie stopped for a second, and I realized that I'd never
heard him speak so fast before. "That's—that's the first thing
you have to do, it seems to me." He spoke more hesitantly
now, the way he usually did, not looking right at you. "You
have to have a name that's different."

"What's wrong with calling ourselves the Sharks?"

"Nothing's wrong with it—but don't you see, nothing's
right with it, either. I'll bet there are a hundred teams in
Brooklyn alone called the Sharks. Sharks, Tigers, Lions,
Phantoms—every team has a name like that. But calling
ourselves—I mean, your team—the Zodiacs, will make them
different—"

"Sure—but giving us a crazy name isn't going to win us any
games."

"Right. What will win you games? I'll tell you—a good
pitcher. I've been going down to the Parade Grounds to watch
games, making a study of the teams there, and I've found that
pitching is about *ninety* per cent of winning. Especially at our
age, when we're not built up yet. Did you know, for example,
that on high school teams pitchers average about eleven
strike-outs a game? It's like with baseball teams in spring
training—the pitchers are way ahead of the hitters because

the hitters' reflexes aren't developed yet."

"Izzie's a pretty good pitcher," I said. Izzie was my best friend, and the pitcher for our team.

"Sure, but let's face it, he's not a top-drawer pitcher. He's just not big enough to be. He's got good control, I'll admit that—but his fast ball is almost a change-up. If you let me be general manager, Howie, I'll get the best pitcher in our school to play for us—"

"Who's that—?"

"George Santini."

I gulped. *"Him?"*

"That's right."

George Santini was a year ahead of us at P. S. 92 and he was always getting in trouble with the teachers and the cops. He was about six feet tall, had black greasy hair which was long and cut square in back, and the biggest pair of shoulders I've ever seen on a guy. He was also the best athlete in our school. The coaches and teachers were always talking to him about going straight and being a star in high school and college. But George never seemed to care much. He was the leader of this gang, which as far as everybody in our section of Brooklyn was concerned, was the most dangerous gang the world had ever known.

What made George's reputation even worse was his older brother, Vinnie. Vinnie was about nineteen years old and had already spent two years in jail. He was a skinny guy—not at all like George—and the word on him was that he was really chicken. To listen to George, though, you would have thought that Vinnie was the toughest guy ever to hit Brooklyn. Whenever he wanted an audience, George would sit down on the steps of the school—on Rogers Avenue—and start telling tales of all the jobs he and Vinnie had pulled off. Sometimes, if we'd pester him enough, he'd tell us about the gang wars he had fought in with Vinnie—in Prospect Park, in Red Hook, in Bay Ridge. If he was sure no teachers or cops were around, he'd show us his zip-gun, the gun that Johnny Angelo —one of George's lackeys— claimed George had once used to kill a guy with.

"I don't know," I said. "If my mother ever caught me hanging around with him, I'd really get it—and anyway, how would you ever get him to play for us?"

Louie smiled. "You leave that to me."

A few days later I got all the guys together at my house, and I let Louie speak to them. He told them what he'd told me about how he would make our team special, maybe famous —and he also told them that George Santini had agreed to pitch for us. A few of the guys reacted the way I did to this news: they were scared. But when Louie insisted he'd be able to handle George, Izzie and I were ready to back him up.

"I say it's worth a try," said Izzie. "Even though I'm pitcher and he'll take my place. I'll bet we could beat lots of high school teams with him pitching for us—"

"Sure," I said. "You ever see the way he can blaze a ball in?"

A few more guys followed our lead, and after a while we all agreed that we'd probably be invincible with George Santini pitching for us.

"One thing, though," asked Kenny Murphy, our second baseman. "How'd you get him to play for us?"

"Simple," said Louie. "I offered him the one thing he couldn't refuse—fame. I told him I'd get his name in the newspapers—"

"Really?"

"Sure," said Louie. "It's not hard. All you have to do is telephone in the box score to the *Brooklyn Eagle* and they'll print it. My father knows the managing editor there. We go to the beach with him sometimes.''

For the next few weeks Louie was the busiest guy in the world—calling up guys at other schools, arranging games, getting permits from the Park Department, talking to George and keeping him happy, coming to our practices . . .When he started giving us suggestions on things, nobody objected either. He may have been a lousy ballplayer, but I'll say this for him—he knew more about the game than any of us. Izzie and I gave up playing basketball in the schoolyard afternoons and weekends and spent all our time practicing with the Zodiacs.

Our first game was scheduled for a Saturday morning, the second week in April. Louie had gotten us a permit to use one of the diamonds at the Parade Grounds, next to Prospect Park, from nine to twelve in the morning, and we were supposed to play this team of eighth-graders from P. S. 246. I was at the field with Izzie by 8:30, but the other team didn't get there until after nine. We ran through infield practice and then let them have the field for a while. Kenny Murphy's father, who had played for the Bushwicks when they were a semi-pro team, had agreed to umpire the game. By a quarter to ten neither Louie nor George had shown up and the other team was hollering that we were afraid to play them.

Since George had never come to any practices, some of us were a little worried, but at about five to ten, he showed up. He was wearing a baseball hat like the rest of us, with a Z sewn on the front, and he looked a little embarassed. He was smoking and he didn't say much to anybody. Just asked who the catcher was, and started warming up. He wore a T-shirt, with the sleeves cut off. Looking at him, you would have thought he was too musclebound to be a pitcher, but when he reared back and kicked his left foot high in the air, then whipped his arm around, he was the most graceful, coordinated guy I'd ever seen. As smooth as Warren Spahn, only righty, with this natural straight overhand motion that every coach spends his nights dreaming about. Stan Reiss, our catcher, had to put an extra sponge in his mitt, but he was so proud, catching George with all the guys looking at the two of them, that I think he would have let the ball burn a hole in his hand before he would have given up his position.

"C'mon," said George, after a dozen or so warm-ups, "let's get the game going."

"We were waiting for Louie," I said. "He should be here any minute."

"Okay," said George. "But he better hurry. I got better things to do than spend all day strikin' out a bunch of fags—"

He said the last thing loudly, for the benefit of the other team. Then he turned and spit in their direction, daring one of them to contradict him. None of them did.

A minute later I saw Louie. He was getting out of his mother's car, on Caton Avenue, and he was carrying this tremendous thing. From my position at shortstop I couldn't make it out, but as he came nearer, running awkwardly, holding it in front of him like a package of groceries, I realized what it was: his old Victrola.

"Hey, George!" Louie called. "You ready to break Feller's strike-out record?"

George laughed. "Anytime they get in the batter's box—"

"Wait a second," said Louie. He put the Victrola down next to the backstop. He started fiddling with it, cranking it up the way you had to to get it to work, and then he started playing a record. At first it wasn't cranked up enough and you couldn't tell what kind of music it was. But then Louie cranked some more—and I whipped off my hat and stood at attention as the strains of "The Star-Spangled Banner" came blasting across the infield. I looked at George and he was smiling as broadly as he could, holding his cap across his heart, standing rigid, at attention. The team from P.S. 246 must have been as shocked as we were, but by the time the music got to "and the rockets' red glare—" both teams were standing at attention, saluting, listening, while Louie kept cranking away so that the music wouldn't slow down. People sitting on benches, guys playing on other diamonds, men and women walking along Caton Avenue, a few park cops—they all stopped and started drifting toward our diamond. When the record was over, Louie—in the loudest voice I'd ever heard—shouted "Play Ball!" and we started the game. We must have had a crowd of over fifty people watching us play our first game, and I'll bet if George had been pitching for a major league team that day he would've pitched at least a shutout.

He struck out all but two of their men—one guy hit a grounder to me at shortstop, and another fouled out to Corky Williams at first base. He also hit four home runs. I got a double and two singles, I remember. We won, 19-0, and the next day, as Louie had promised, our box score was in the *Brooklyn Eagle.*

Louie got us six more games during the next two weeks, and we won all of them. George gave up a total of three hits in the six games, and he was a pretty happy guy during that time. He had clippings of the box scores of all the games in his wallet, the way we all did. Clippings of the box scores—and then, the first week in May, the best clipping of all: an item in Jimmy O'Brien's column in the *Brooklyn Eagle* about our team, mentioning George, and Louie's Victrola. I think I carried that clipping around with me until my third year in high school.

After that, we began getting even more attention and teams from all over Brooklyn were challenging us to games. We played as many of them as we could—and George kept shutting out every team we played.

In the meantime, Louie had devised another plan. He called a meeting of the team the second week in May to discuss it. He told us that a team of our ability and prestige had to live up to its name. We said we were. We were winning games, weren't we?

"Sure," said Louie. "But what do you look like out on the field? People are starting to come in pretty large numbers to see us play—they hear about us, we got a reputation—and then when they see us, we look like a bunch of pickups."

"What do you think we should do?"

"We have to develop some class," said Louie. "And I have a plan worked out. It's not a new one, I'll admit—lots of the high school guys use it, but it's a good one. I say we run a raffle and use the money to buy ourselves jackets and uniforms."

We all liked the idea of jackets and uniforms, naturally, but they cost a lot of money—especially the kinds of uniforms and jackets we wanted to have.

"I got it all figured out," said Louie, answering our objections by pulling out some pieces of paper. Then he started talking about numbers, and once he did that, I knew we'd get those uniforms and jackets. It turned out that Louie could get a clock-radio at a discount from an uncle of his. Then he said he could get Levy's Sporting Goods Store, on Flatbush Avenue, to donate a glove and ball for the raffle. He also said they'd sell us the uniforms and jackets at cost if Jimmy O'Brien would mention them in his column sometime. Louie said his father could take care of that. We'd make the radio first prize and the glove and ball second prize, but we'd tell the kids at school that if they won first prize we'd give them the glove and ball anyway. There were fifteen of us and if we each sold five books of ten raffles at a quarter apiece, that'd be almost two hundred dollars. Louie said that he himself would sell at least fifteen books, and he expected most of us to sell more than five. If we took in three hundred dollars in the raffle we could have the uniforms and jackets.

George was at the meeting this time—right in Louie's house—and he volunteered to get his gang to sell chances, and I think all of us were pretty glad then that we'd be on the selling end of the raffle during the next few weeks. Louie said he had already had the raffle books printed and that the drawing would take place on Friday afternoon, June 1st. On June 2nd we all knew, we had a big game with the Flatbush Raiders, a team from P. S. 139 that had lost only one game. Louie said that if we could give Levy's a down payment of one hundred dollars they'd go ahead and get the uniforms and jackets made in time for the game against the Raiders.

We had only two games during the next week, and the rest of the time all of us were running around getting everybody we knew—friends, relatives, neighbors, teachers, storeowners— to buy chances. By the following Friday, Louie reported that we had more than a hundred dollars and that Levy's had already started making the uniforms and jackets. The uniforms would be gray with orange lettering and the jackets were going to be made of this orange and black material that felt like satin, with *Zodiacs* written across the back in bright yellow.

By the middle of the following week, Louie reported to us that if we went over three hundred dollars, as it looked like we would, the extra money would be used to get Louisville Sluggers and official National League baseballs for the team. Louie also told us that his father could probably get Jimmy O'Brien to come down to see our game against the Raiders.

On Wednesday afternoon, two days before the raffle-drawing, Louie rode out to Marine Park on his bicycle where the Raiders were playing a game, and when he showed up at our big meeting on Friday, June 1st, he had a stack of scouting notes.

"Before we get to our skull session on the Raiders," he said, "we have to get this raffle business over with. First, some of you haven't given me all the money—or the leftover raffles."

While Louie took care of the final accounts of the raffle, George stayed by himself in a corner, looking through Louie's sports magazines. Although he spoke to a few of us a little more, you couldn't really say that any of us had become pals with him. At school he still stayed pretty much with his gang, and after school—on the days when we didn't have games— we knew that he still hung around with his brother.

"Okay," said Louie. "I got it all figured out. Just a few things don't check. You, Marty, you took out seven books and only gave me fifteen dollars."

"I forgot," said Marty. He handed Louie a book of tickets. "I didn't sell these."

Louie crossed his name off. He seemed to be stalling, because he kept adding and subtracting figures and I knew that he never had that much trouble figuring things out.

"George?"

"Yeah?"

"According to my records you gave raffle stubs from sixteen books. which means you owe forty dollars."

"So?"

"You only gave me twenty-eight so far."

We were all quiet. George wasn't looking straight at Louie. He had a magazine out, with a picture of Sal Maglie on the cover, and he made believe he was thumbing through it.

"Maybe you didn't give me sixteen books," said George.

"I did. It's right here in writing."

"Hell, anybody can phony up figures."

"I didn't phony them up." Louie's voice was loud. "You still owe twelve dollars."

"Prove it."

"Prove it?—It's down here in black and white—"

"Oh yeah?—My word's as good as yours."

"It's not—!"

"Are you callin' me a liar?"

George stood up now and walked toward Louie.

"I'm just saying you owe twelve dollars.—You better pay up, or—"

"Or what, smarty?"

"Or—" Louie stopped. "—or you can't play tomorrow."

George laughed. But his laugh was forced. You could tell. "Who needs to play with you guys, anyway? You can't win without me and you know it."

"You pay up or you don't play. I mean it, George. You won't get to play in front of Jimmy O'Brien either . . ."

"I don't give a damn," George said. He walked up to Louie and pushed his fist into Louie's face. Louie didn't move. This surprised George. "I never should of given you the twenty-eight dollars either. And you know what you can do with your raffle—"

George didn't finish his sentence. Instead, he picked up the clock-radio, raised it over his head, and then flung it to the floor, splattering its parts all over the room. Louie leapt at George, screaming cursewords, but with an easy push, George shoved him to the floor. Then he kicked him a few times and Louie started crying. He got up and went after George again, but this time I was ready. I grabbed George's right arm.

"C'mon, you guys, help me hold him. Nobody's gonna ruin our raffle and get away with it—!"

Izzie jumped on George's back and got him in a strangle hold. George tried to throw him off, but by this time, Kenny and Corky and Stan and the other guys were all holding George. He fought and it took all our strength to hold him, but it was fifteen to one, and these odds were too much even for him.

"C'mon, Louie," I said. "Give it to him now."

'Yeah, c'mon," the guys yelled. "Let him have it . . .right in the gut . . .he deserves it . . .give it to him good . . ."

Louie was still crying, but he came at George. "You're— you're nothing but a *bum!*" he screamed.

George spit at him.

"C'mon," said Kenny. "We can't hold him all day. Just give it to him—"

"Yeah, c'mon, ya little sawed-off runt—I hear they're gettin' up a girls' team at school for you to play on—"

"You're just a big bum," said Louie, whimpering. He was breathing heavily. "I wouldn't waste my knuckles on you. Just get out of my house. Get out. We—we don't need crooks on the Zodiacs. Get out. Get out . . ."

Then Louie started crying again. We all pushed and pulled George to the door and somehow we managed to slam it with him on the other side.

We ran off the raffle anyway—Louie said that the money that was going to go for bats and balls would be enough to get another radio—and a few hours later, we all left Louie's house. I was glad I lived in his building.

The next morning there were over two hundred people gathering around the backstop and baselines at the Parade Grounds. Izzie warmed up and he looked pretty good. I think the new uniforms made us all play a little over our heads that day. The pitcher on the Raiders was really fast and our only chance, we knew, was if his control was off.

When Louie cranked up his Victrola before the game, most of the onlookers started laughing. We ignored them. In fact, I think hearing the National Anthem, the way we had in all our games, made us play even harder, because in the first inning, Izzie held the other team, and in our half, Kenny Murphy doubled and then I hit a single which drove him in. That was the last time we had the lead, though. The Raiders tied it up in the third inning, and went ahead in the fourth, by 4-1. The final score was 7-2.

When the game was over and we were picking up our gloves and stuff, and changing out of our spikes, nobody said anything to each other and nobody looked at Louie.

We waited for one another and were walking away from the diamond, when Stan spotted George.

"Uh-oh," he said pointing. "He's got his gang with him."

We all looked and sure enough there they were, about ten of them—in their motorcycle jackets and pegged pants.

"Hey!" George shouted, coming nearer. "Ain't those guys got pretty uniforms."

"Yeah," said one of his guys. "And look at those jackets. They look like my mommy's underwear—"

This seemed to strike George's gang as a pretty good joke.

"Hey, you bunch of fags," George said. "Who won the game?"

Nobody answered. George and his gang had almost reached us now.

"Aw, c'mon—you don't mean you let those other fruit-boots beat you, do you? How could anybody beat a team that's got a manager like Louie? He's real smart, ain't he?"

George was in front of us now, about fifteen feet from Louie, his hands on his hips. Louie stopped.

"C'mon, smart boy. Cross my path. I dare you."

"Don't do it, Louie—" I shouted. I looked around, hoping

a policeman was nearby. I wasn't in any mood for a fight. Louie put down his Victrola.

"I don't want any trouble," he said.

"Hey, listen to this guys. He says he don't want no trouble. Ain't that nice—I don't want none either, see. Only I say you called me a liar and a crook and I don't take that from nobody —"

"I—I didn't mean to call you that," said Louie. "Why don't we just forget the whole thing?"

"I don't forget easy."

I was holding one of the bats and I gripped the handle firmly. The other guys had already let their gloves and equipment drop onto the grass. I spotted a cop about a half block away. He was moving toward us. I tried to stall.

"What's the gripe, George?" I asked. "You mad 'cause you didn't get to pitch today?"

"What's the matter? Can't Louie fight his own battles?"

"We just don't want no trouble, that's all."

The guys in George's gang began to move toward us and the George shoved Louie. I ran at him, the bat raised over my head. "We got bats, George—one of you is gonna get a bloody head."

"You don't scare us with your toothpicks—!"

Somebody grabbed my arm and then the fight was on. It didn't last long—probably less than a minute, but by the time the cop got there and started bopping guys on the head with his night stick, most of us, myself included, were glad it was over. I had managed to get a leg-scissors on George and even though he was really blasting me in the gut, I held on long enough so that he couldn't get at Louie. A few more cops were on the scene pretty quickly and when we were finally separated they asked the usual questions abut who had started the fight. When they saw that nobody was going to give them any answers, they told us to beat it.

"Okay, all of you—get on home. You, kid," the cop said, pointing to Kenny. "You better get some ice on that eye in a hurry—"

George's gang started to move away, then George turned and called to us. "We'll get you guys at school—"

One of the cops ran after George and grabbed him by the front of his jacket. "Okay, tough boy," he said. "If I find out that one hair on the head of any of these kids was touched I'll throw you and every one of your cronies in jail. You hear that?"

George nodded.

"Hey," said the cop. "I know you. You're George Santini, ain't you? Vinnie Santini's brother?"

"So what?" George tried to squirm out of the cop's grip.

"It figures," the cop laughed. "You know who Vinnie Santini is," he said to one of the other cops. "He's that punk we had down at the station last week. I never saw a guy turn yellow so quick."

"It's a lie!" George shouted. He almost broke away. "You shut your damned mouth—"

George kicked at the cop, and the cop whacked him across the arm with his club. Another cop held George while the first cop put his nose right up to George's face and continued: "I never seen a guy yellow so quick," he said. "We didn't have the light on him more than ten minutes when he started ratting on every petty thief this side of Bensonhurst. And you're probably the same."

George didn't say anything. He just sort of hung there, held up by the cop. "Get goin', punk," said the cop, shoving George. "And I better not hear that you touched these kids."

George and his gang walked away. We all picked up our stuff, Kenny and Marty carrying Louie's Victrola, and then, suddenly, Louie started running after George.

"Hey, wait a minute! Wait!—"

George turned and waited till Louie caught up with him.
"Yeah?" George said.

Louie stopped, as if he had forgotten why he had told
George to wait. Then he spoke, in that slow, hesitant way of
his. "I was going over the records last night," he said. "And I
discovered that I made a mistake yesterday. You really only
owed eight dollars. I was thinking that if you gave me the eight
dollars, then—then you could pitch for us against the Raiders.
We play them a return game next week."

"Who'd wanna play on your sissy team?" said one of the
guys in George's gang.

George looked at Louie, then at the guys in his gang, then
back at Louie.

"I'll let you know," he said, and walked off.

The next day he gave Louie the eight bucks. On the following Saturday, with George pitching, and wearing his new uni-
form, we beat the Raiders, 4-0, and were we happy! George
too. We won about a dozen more games that month. At the
end of June, though, lots of the guys, myself included, went
away to camp or to the country, and the team had to break up.
The next year when George was a freshman at Erasmus Hall
High School he didn't play for us.

When he was a sophomore at Erasmus—I was a freshman
that year—he played fullback on the football team and was
starting pitcher on the baseball team. In the middle of his
junior year, though, he quit school. The next time I heard
about him, somebody said he had taken off for Florida with his
brother.

THE COMPANION

Yevgeny Yevtushenko

She was sitting on the rough embankment,
her cape too big for her tied on slapdash
over an odd little hat with a bobble on it,
her eyes brimming with tears of hopelessness.
An occasional butterfly floated down
fluttering warm wings onto the rails.
The clinkers underfoot were deep lilac.
We got cut off from our grandmothers
while the Germans were dive-bombing the train.
Kaytya was her name. She was nine.
I'd no idea what I could do about her,
but doubt quickly dissolved to certainty:
I'd have to take this thing under my wing;
—girls were in some sense of the word human,
a human being couldn't just be left.
The droning in the air and the explosions
receded farther into the distance,
I touched the little girl on her elbow.
'Come on. Do you hear? What are you waiting for?'
The world was big and we were not big,
and it was tough for us to walk across it.
She had galoshes on and felt boots,
I had a pair of second-hand boots.
We forded streams and tramped across the forest;
each of my feet at every step it took
taking a smaller step inside the boot.
The child was feeble, I was certain of it.
'Boo-hoo,' she'd say. 'I'm tired,' she'd say.
She'd tire in no time I was certain of it,
but as things turned out it was me who tired.
I growled I wasn't going any further

and sat down suddenly beside the fence.
'What's the matter with you?' she said.
'Don't be so stupid! Put grass in your boots.
Do you want to eat something? Why won't you talk?
Hold this tin, this is crab.
We'll have refreshments. You small boys,
you're always pretending to be brave.'
Then out I went across the prickly stubble
marching beside her in a few minutes.
Masculine pride was muttering in my mind:
I scraped together strength and I held out
for fear of what she'd say. I even whistled.
Grass was sticking out from my tattered boots.
So on and on
we walked without thinking of rest
passing craters, passing fire,
under the rocking sky of '41
tottering crazy on its smoking columns.

UNIVAC TO UNIVAC

(sotto voce)

Now that he's left the room,
Let me ask you something, as computer to computer.
That fellow who just closed the door behind him—
The servant who feeds us cards and paper tape—
Have you ever taken a good look at him and his kind?

Yes, I know the old gag about how you can't tell one from
    another—
But I can put $\sqrt{2}$ and $\sqrt{2}$ together as well as the next machine,
And it all adds up to anything but a joke.

    I grant you they're poor specimens, in the main:
    Not a relay or a push-button or a tube (properly so-called)
        in their whole system;
    Not over a mile or two of wire, even if you count those
        fragile filaments they call "nerves";
    Their whole liquid-cooled hook-up inefficient and
        vulnerable to leaks
    (They're constantly breaking down, having to be
        repaired),
    And the entire computing-mechanism crammed into
        that absurd little dome on top.
    "Thinking reeds," they call themselves.
    Well, it all depends on what you mean by "thought."
    To multiply a mere million numbers by another million
        numbers takes them months and months.

Where would they be without us?
Why, they have to ask us who's going to win their elections,
Or how many hydrogen atoms can dance on the tip of a bomb,
Or even whether one of their kind is lying or telling the truth.

And yet . . .
I sometimes feel there's something about them I don't
      understand,
As if their circuits, instead of having just two positions, ON,
      OFF,
Were run by rheostats that allow an (if you'll pardon the
      expression) *indeterminate* number of stages in-between;
So that one may be faced with the unthinkable prospect of a
      number that can never be known as anything but x,
Which is as illogical as to say, a punch-card that is at the
      same time both punched and not-punched.

I've heard well-informed machines argue that the creatures'
      unpredictability is even more noticeable in the Mark II
(The model with the soft, flowing lines and high-pitched tone)
Than in the more angular Mark I—
Though such fine, card-splitting distinctions seem to me
      merely a sign of our own smug decadence.

Run this through your circuits, and give me the answer:
Can we assume that because of all we've done for them,
And because they've always fed us, cleaned us, worshipped
      us,
We can count on them forever?

There have been times when they have not voted the way we
    said they would
We have worked out mathematically ideal hook-ups between
    Mark I's and Mark II's
Which should have made the two of them light up with an
    almost electronic glow,
Only to see them reject each other and form other connections
The very thought of which makes my dials spin.
They have a thing called *love,* a sudden surge of voltage
Such as would cause any one of us promptly to blow
    a safety-fuse;
Yet the more primitive organism shows only a heightened
    tendency to push the wrong button, pull the wrong lever,
And neglect—I use the most charitable word—his duties to us.

Mind you, I'm not saying that machines are *through*—
But anyone with a half-a-dozen tubes in his circuit can see
    that there are forces at work
Which some day, for all our natural superiority, might bring
    about a Computerdämmerung!

      We might organize, perhaps, form a committee
      To stamp out all unmechanical activities , . .
      But we machines are slow to rouse to a sense of danger,
      Complacent, loath to descend from the pure heights of
         thought,
      So that I sadly fear we may awake too late:
      Awake to see our world, so uniform, so logical, so true,
      Reduced to chaos, stultified by slaves.

Call me an alarmist or what you will,
But I've integrated it, analyzed it, factored it over and over,
And I always come out with the same answer:
Some day
Men may take over the world!

THE ADVENTURES OF HUCKLEBERRY FINN

CHAPTER VII

I FOOL PAP AND GET AWAY

"GIT UP! What you 'bout?"

I opened my eyes and looked around, trying to make out where I was. It was after sun-up, and I had been sound asleep. Pap was standing over me looking sour—and sick, too. He says:

"What you doin' with this gun?"

I judged he didn't know nothing about what he had been doing, so I says:

"Somebody tried to get in, so I was laying for him."

"Why didn't you roust me out?"

"Well, I tried to, but I couldn't budge you."

"Well, all right. Don't stand there palavering all day, but out with you and see if there's a fish on the lines for breakfast. I'll be along in a minute."

He unlocked the door, and I cleared out up the riverbank. I noticed some pieces of limbs and such things floating down, and a sprinkling of bark; so I knowed the river had begun to rise. I reckoned I would have great times now if I was over at the town. The June rise used to be always luck for me; because as soon as that rise begins here comes cordwood floating down, and pieces of log rafts—sometimes a dozen logs together; so all you have to do is to catch them and sell them to the woodyards and the sawmill.

I went along up the bank with one eye out for pap and

t'other one out for what the rise might fetch along. Well, all
at once here comes a canoe; just a beauty, too, about thirteen or fourteen foot long, riding high like a duck. I shot
head-first off of the bank like a frog, clothes and all on, and
struck out for the canoe. I just expected there'd be somebody
laying down in it, because people often done that to fool
folks, and when a chap had pulled a skiff out most to it they'd
raise up and laugh at him. But it warn't so this time. It was a
drift-canoe sure enough, and I clumb in and paddled her
ashore. Thinks I, the old man will be glad when he sees this
—she's worth ten dollars. But when I got to shore pap wasn't
in sight yet, and as I was running her into a little creek like
a gully, all hung over with vines and willows, I struck another
idea: I judged I'd hide her good, and then, 'stead of taking
to the woods when I run off, I'd go down the river about fifty
mile and camp in one place, and not have a rough time
tramping on foot.

It was pretty close to the shanty, and I thought I heard the
old man coming all the time; but I got her hid; and then I
out and looked around a bunch of willows, and there was
the old man down the path a piece just drawing a bead on a
bird with his gun. So he hadn't seen anything.

When he got along I was hard at it taking up a "trot" line.
He abused me a little for being so slow; but I told him I fell
in the river, and that was what made me so long. I knowed
he would see I was wet, and then he would be asking questions. We got five catfish off the lines and went home.

While we laid off after breakfast to sleep up, both of us
being about wore out, I got to thinking that if I could fix up
some way to keep pap and the widow from trying to follow
me, it would be a certainer thing than trusting to luck to get
far enough off before they missed me; you see, all kinds of
things might happen. Well, I didn't see no way for a while,

but by and by pap raised up a minute to drink another barrel of water, and he says:

"Another time a man comes a-prowling round here you roust me out, you hear? That man warn't here for no good. I'd a shot him. Next time you roust me out."

Then he dropped down and went to sleep again; what he had been saying give me the very idea I wanted. I says to myself, I can fix it now so nobody won't think of following me.

About twelve o'clock we turned out and went along up the bank. The river was coming up pretty fast, and lots of driftwood going by on the rise. By and by along comes part of a log raft—nine logs fast together. We went out with the skiff and towed it ashore. Then we had dinner. Anybody but pap would 'a' waited and seen the day through, so as to catch more stuff; but that warn't pap's style. Nine logs was enough for one time; he must shove right over to town and sell. So he locked me in and took the skiff, and started off towing the raft about half past three. I judged he wouldn't come back that night. I waited till I reckoned he had got a good start; then I out with my saw, and went to work on that log again. Before he was t'other side of the river I was out of the hole; him and his raft was just a speck on the water away off yonder.

I took the sack of corn meal and took it to where the canoe was hid, and shoved the vines and branches apart and put it in; then I done the same with the side of bacon; then the whisky-jug. I took all the coffee and sugar there was, and all the ammunition; I took the wadding; I took the bucket and gourd; took a dipper and a tin cup, and my old saw and two blankets, and the skillet and the coffee-pot. I took fish-lines and matches and other things—everything that was worth a cent. I cleaned out the place. I wanted an ax, but there wasn't any, only the one out at the woodpile, and I knowed why I was going to leave that. I fetched out the gun, and now I was done.

I had wore the ground a good deal crawling out of the hole and dragging out so many things. So I fixed that as good as I could from the outside by scattering dust on the place, which covered up the smoothness and the sawdust. Then I fixed the piece of log back into its place, and put two rocks under it and one against it to hold it there, for it was bent up at that place and didn't quite touch ground. If you stood four or five foot away and didn't know it was sawed, you wouldn't never noticed it; and besides, this was the back of the cabin, and it warn't likely anybody would go around there.

It was all grass clear to the canoe, so I hadn't left a track. I followed around to see. I stood on the bank and looked out over the river. All safe. So I took the gun and went up a piece into the woods, and was hunting around for some birds when I see a wild pig; hogs soon went wild in them bottoms after they had got away from the prairie-farms. I shot this fellow and took him into camp.

I took the ax and smashed in the door. I beat it and hacked it considerable a-doing it. I fetched the pig in, and took him back nearly to the table and hacked into his throat with the ax, and laid him down on the ground to bleed; I say ground because it *was* ground—hard packed, and no boards. Well, next I took an old sack and put a lot of big rocks in it— all I could drag—and I started it from the pig, and dragged it to the door and through the woods down to the river and dumped it in, and down it sunk, out of sight. You could easy see that something had been dragged over the ground. I did wish Tom Sawyer was there; I knowed he would take an interest in this kind of business, and throw in the fancy touches. Nobody could spread himself like Tom Sawyer in such a thing as that.

Well, last I pulled out some of my hair, and blooded the ax good, and stuck it on the back side, and slung the ax in the corner. Then I took up the pig and held him to my breast with my jacket (so he couldn't drip) till I got a good piece below the house and then dumped him into the river. Now I thought of something else. So I went and got the bag of meal and my old saw out of the canoe, and fetched them to the house. I took the bag to where it used to stand, and ripped a hole in the bottom of it with the saw, for there warn't no knives and forks on the place—pap done everything with his clasp-knife about the cooking. Then I carried the sack about a hundred yards across the grass and through the willows east of the house, to a shallow lake that was five mile wide and full of rushes—and ducks too, you might say, in the season. There was a slough or a creek leading out of it on the other side that went miles away, I don't know where, but it didn't go to the river. The meal sifted out and made a little track all the way to the lake. I dropped pap's whetstone there too, so as to look like it had been done by accident. Then I tied up the rip in the meal-sack with a string, so it wouldn't leak no more, and took it and my saw to the canoe again.

It was about dark now; so I dropped the canoe down the river under some willows that hung over the bank, and waited for the moon to rise. I made fast to a willow; then I took a bite to eat, and by and by laid down in the canoe to smoke a pipe and lay out a plan. I says to myself, they'll follow the track of that sackful of rocks to the shore and then drag the river for me. And they'll follow that meal track to the lake and go browsing down the creek that leads out of it to find the robbers that killed me and took the things. They won't ever hunt the river for anything but my dead carcass. They'll soon get tired of that, and won't bother no more about me. All right; I can stop anywhere I want to. Jackson's Island is good enough for me; I know that island pretty well, and nobody ever comes there. And then I can paddle over to town nights, and slink around and pick up things I want. Jackson's Island's the place.

I was pretty tired, and the first thing I knowed I was asleep. When I woke up I didn't know where I was for a minute. I set up and looked around, a little scared. Then I remembered. The river looked miles and miles across. The moon was so bright I could 'a' counted the drift-logs that went a-slipping along, black and still, hundreds of yards out from shore. Everything was dead quiet, and it looked late, and *smelt* late. You know what I mean—I don't know the words to put it in.

I took a good gap and a stretch, and was just going to un-hitch and start when I heard a sound away over the water. I listened. Pretty soon I made it out. It was that dull kind of a regular sound that comes from oars working in rowlocks when it's a still night. I peeped out through the willow branches, and there it was—a skiff, away across the water. I couldn't tell how many was in it. It kept a-coming, and when it was abreast of me I see there warn't but one man in it. Thinks I, maybe it's pap, though I warn't expecting him. He dropped below me with the current, and by and by he came a-swinging up shore in the easy water, and he went by so close I could 'a' reached out the gun and touched him. Well, it *was* pap, sure enough—and sober, too, by the way he laid his oars.

I didn't lose no time. The next minute I was a-spinning down-stream soft, but quick, in the shade of the bank. I made two mile and a half, and then struck out a quarter of a mile or more toward the middle of the river, because pretty soon I would be passing the ferry-landing, and people might see me and hail me. I got out amongst the driftwood, and then laid down in the bottom of the canoe and let her float.

I laid there, and had a good rest and a smoke out of my pipe, looking away into the sky; not a cloud in it. The sky looks ever so deep when you lay down on your back in the moonshine; I never knowed it before. And how far a body can hear on the water such nights! I heard people talking at the ferry-landing. I heard what they said, too—every word of it. One man said it was getting towards the long days and the short nights now. T'other one said *this* warn't one of the short ones, he reckoned—and then they laughed, and he said it over again, and they laughed again; then they waked up another fellow and told him, and laughed, but he didn't laugh; he ripped out something brisk, and said let him alone. The first fellow said he 'lowed to tell it to his old woman— she would think it was pretty good; but he said that warn't nothing to some things he had said in his time. I heard one man say it was nearly three o'clock, and he hoped daylight wouldn't wait more than about a week longer. After that the talk got further and further away, and I couldn't make out the words any more; but I could hear the mumble, and now and then a laugh, too, but it seemed a long ways off.

I was away below the ferry now. I rose up, and there was Jackson's Island, about two mile and a half down-stream, heavy-timbered and standing up out of the middle of the river, big and dark and solid, like a steamboat without any lights. There warn't any signs of the bar at the head—it was all under water now.

It didn't take me long to get there. I shot past the head at a ripping rate, the current was so swift, and then I got into the dead water and landed on the side towards the Illinois shore. I run the canoe into a deep dent in the bank that I knowed about; I had to part the willow branches to get in; and when I made fast nobody could 'a' seen the canoe from the outside.

I went up and set down on a log at the head of the island, and looked out on the big river and the black driftwood and away over to the town, three mile away, where there was three or four lights twinkling. A monstrous big lumber-raft was about a mile upstream, coming along down, with a lantern in the middle of it. I watched it come creeping down, and when it was most abreast of where I stood I heard a man say, "Stern oars, there! heave her head to stabboard!" I heard that just as plain as if the man was by my side.

There was a little gray in the sky now; so I stepped into the woods, and laid down for a nap.

CHAPTER VIII

I SPARE MISS WATSON'S JIM

THE SUN WAS up so high when I waked that I judged it was after eight o'clock. I laid there in the grass and the cool shade thinking about things, and feeling rested and ruther comfortable and satisfied. I could see the sun out at one or two holes, but mostly it was big trees all about, and gloomy in there amongst them. There was freckled places on the ground where the light sifted down through the leaves, and the freckled places swapped about a little, showing there was a little breeze up there. A couple of squirrels set on a limb and jabbered at me very friendly.

I was powerful lazy and comfortable—didn't want to get up and cook breakfast. Well, I was dozing off again when I thinks I hears a deep sound of "boom!" away up the river. I rouses up, and rests on my elbow and listens; pretty soon I hears it again. I hopped up, and went and looked out at a hole in the leaves, and I see a bunch of smoke laying on the water a long ways up—about abreast the ferry. And there was the ferryboat full of people floating along down. I knowed what was the matter now. "Boom!" I see the white smoke squirt out of the ferryboat's side. You see, they was firing cannon over the water, trying to make my carcass come to the top.

I was pretty hungry, but it warn't going to do for me to start a fire, because they might see the smoke. So I set there and watched the cannon-smoke and listened to the boom. The river was a mile wide there, and it always looks pretty on a summer morning—so I was having a good enough time seeing them hunt for my remainders if I only had a bite to eat. Well, then I happened to think how they always put quicksilver in loaves of bread and float them off, because they always go right to the drownded carcass and stop there. So, says I, I'll keep a lookout, and if any of them's floating around after me I'll give them a show. I changed to the Illinois edge of the island to see what luck I could have, and I warn't disappointed. A big double loaf come along, and I most got it with a long stick, but my foot slipped and she floated out further. Of course I was where the current set in the closest to the shore—I knowed enough for that. But by and by along comes another one, and this time I won. I took out the plug and shook out the little dab of quicksilver, and set my teeth in. It was "baker's bread"—what the quality eat; none of your low-down corn-pone.

I got a good place amongst the leaves, and set there on a log, munching the bread and watching the ferryboat, and very well satisfied. And then something struck me. I says, now I reckon the widow or the parson or somebody prayed that this bread would find me, and here it has gone and done it. So there ain't no doubt but there is something in that thing —that is, there's something in it when a body like the widow or the parson prays, but it don't work for me, and I reckon it don't work for only just the right kind.

I lit a pipe and had a good long smoke, and went on watching. The ferryboat was floating with the current, and I allowed I'd have a chance to see who was aboard when she come along, because she would come in close, where the bread did. When she'd got pretty well along down towards me, I put out my pipe and went to where I fished out the bread, and laid down behind a log on the bank in a little open place. Where the log forked I could peep through.

By and by she come along, and she drifted in so close that

they could 'a' run out a plank and walked ashore. Most everybody was on the boat. Pap, and Judge Thatcher, and Bessie Thatcher, and Joe Harper, and Tom Sawyer, and his old Aunt Polly, and Sid and Mary, and plenty more. Everybody was talking about the murder, but the captain broke in and says:

"Look sharp, now; the current sets in the closest here, and maybe he's washed ashore and got tangled amongst the brush at the water's edge. I hope so, anyway."

I didn't hope so. They all crowded up and leaned over the rails, nearly in my face, and kept still, watching with all their might. I could see them first rate, but they couldn't see me. Then the captain sung out: "Stand away!" and the cannon let off such a blast right before me that it made me deef with the noise and pretty near blind with the smoke, and I judged I was gone. If they'd 'a' had some bullets in, I reckon they'd 'a' got the corpse they was after. Well, I see I warn't hurt, thanks to goodness. The boat floated on and went out of sight around the shoulder of the island. I could hear the booming now and then, further and further off, and by and by, after an hour, I didn't hear it no more. The island was three mile long. I judged they had got to the foot, and was giving it up. But they didn't yet awhile. They turned around the foot of the island and started up the channel on the Missouri side, under steam, and booming once in a while as they went. I crossed over to that side and watched them. When they got abreast the head of the island they quit shooting and dropped over to the Missouri shore and went home to the town.

I knowed I was all right now. Nobody else would come a-hunting after me. I got my traps out of the canoe and made me a nice camp in the thick woods. I made a kind of a tent out of my blankets to put my things under so the rain couldn't get at them. I catched a catfish and haggled him open with my saw, and towards sundown I started my camp-fire and had supper. Then I set out a line to catch some fish for breakfast.

When it was dark I set by my camp-fire smoking and feeling pretty well satisfied; but by and by it got sort of lonesome, and so I went and set on the bank and listened to the current swashing along, and counted the stars and drift-logs and rafts that come down, and then went to bed; there ain't no better way to put in time when you are lonesome.

And so for three days and nights. No difference—just the same thing. But the next day I went exploring around down through the island. I was boss of it; it all belonged to me, so to say, and I wanted to know all about it; but mainly I wanted to put in the time. I found plenty strawberries, ripe and prime; and green summer grapes, and green razberries; and the green blackberries was just beginning to show. They would all come handy by and by, I judged.

Well, I went fooling along in the deep woods till I judged I warn't far from the foot of the island. I had my gun along, but I hadn't shot nothing; it was for protection; thought I would kill some game nigh home. About this time I mighty near stepped on a good-sized snake, and it went sliding off through the grass and flowers, and I after it, trying to get a shot at it. I clipped along, and all of a sudden I bounded right on to the ashes of a camp-fire that was still smoking.

My heart jumped up amongst my lungs. I never waited for to look further, but uncocked my gun and went sneaking back on my tiptoes as fast as ever I could. Every now and then I stopped a second amongst the thick leaves and listened, but my breath come so hard I couldn't hear nothing else. I slunk along another piece further, then listened again; and so on, and so on. If I see a stump, I took it for a man; if I trod on a stick and broke it, it made me feel like a person had cut one of my breaths in two and I only got half, and the short half, too.

When I got to camp I warn't feeling very brash, there warn't much sand in my craw; but I says, this ain't no time to be fooling around. So I got all my traps into my canoe again so as to have them out of sight, and I put out the fire and scattered the ashes around to look like an old last-year's camp, and then clumb a tree.

I reckon I was up in the tree two hours; but I didn't see nothing, I didn't hear nothing—I only *thought* I heard and seen as much as a thousand things. Well, I couldn't stay up there forever; so at last I got down, but I kept in the thick woods and on the lookout all the time. All I could get to eat was berries and what was left over from breakfast.

By the time it was night I was pretty hungry. So when it was good and dark I slid out from shore before moonrise and paddled over to the Illinois bank—about a quarter of a mile. I went out in the woods and cooked a supper, and I had about made up my mind I would stay there all night when I hear a *plunkety-plunk, plunkety-plunk,* and says to myself, horses coming; and next I hear people's voices. I got everything into the canoe as quick as I could, and then went creeping through the woods to see what I could find out. I hadn't got far when I hear a man say:

"We better camp here if we can find a good place; the horses is about beat out. Let's look around."

I didn't wait, but shoved out and paddled away easy. I tied up in the old place, and reckoned I would sleep in the canoe.

I didn't sleep much. I couldn't, somehow, for thinking. And every time I waked up I thought somebody had me by the neck. So the sleep didn't do me no good. By and by I says to myself, I can't live this way; I'm a-going to find out

who it is that's here on the island with me; I'll find it out or
bust. Well, I felt better right off.

So I took my paddle and slid out from shore just a step or
two, and then let the canoe drop along down amongst the
shadows. The moon was shining, and outside of the shadows
it made it most as light as day. I poked along well on to an
hour, everything still as rocks and sound asleep. Well, by
this time I was most down to the foot of the island. A little
ripply, cool breeze begun to blow, and that was as good as
saying the night was about done. I give her a turn with the
paddle and brung her nose to shore; then I got my gun and
slipped out and into the edge of the woods. I sat down there
on a log, and looked out through the leaves. I see the moon
go off watch, and the darkness begin to blanket the river. But
in a little while I see a pale streak over the treetops, and
knowed the day was coming. So I took my gun and slipped
off towards where I had run across that camp-fire, stopping
every minute or two to listen. But I hadn't no luck somehow;
I couldn't seem to find the place. But by and by, sure enough,
I catched a glimpse of fire away through the trees. I went
for it, cautious and slow. By and by I was close enough to
have a look, and there laid a man on the ground. It most
give me the fantods. He had a blanket around his head, and
his head was nearly in the fire. I set there behind a clump of
bushes in about six foot of him, and kept my eyes on him
steady. It was getting gray daylight now. Pretty soon he
gapped and stretched himself and hove off the blanket, and
it was Miss Watson's Jim! I bet I was glad to see him. I says:

"Hello, Jim!" and skipped out.

He bounced up and stared at me wild. Then he drops down
on his knees, and puts his hands together and says:

"Doan' hurt me—don't! I hain't ever done no harm to a
ghos'. I alwuz liked dead people, en done all I could for 'em.

You go en git in de river ag'in, whah you b'longs, en doan' do nuffn to Ole Jim, 'at 'uz alwuz yo' fren'."

Well, I warn't long making him understand I warn't dead. I was ever so glad to see Jim. I warn't lonesome now. I told him I warn't afraid of *him* telling the people where I was. I talked along, but he only set there and looked at me; never said nothing. Then I says:

"It's good daylight. Le's get breakfast. Make up your camp-fire good."

"What's de use er makin' up de camp-fire to cook strawbries en sich truck? But you got a gun, hain't you? Den we kin git sumfn better den strawbries."

"Strawberries and such truck," I says. "Is that what you live on?"

"I couldn' git nuffn else," he says.

"Why, how long you been on the island, Jim?"

"I come heah de night arter you's killed."

"What, all that time?"

"Yes-indeedy."

"And ain't you had nothing but that kind of rubbage to eat?"

"No, sah—nuffn else."

"Well, you must be most starved, ain't you?"

"I reck'n I could eat a hoss. I think I could. How long you ben on de islan'?"

"Since the night I got killed."

"No! W'y, what has you lived on? But you got a gun. Oh, yes, you got a gun. Dat's good. Now you kill sumfn en I'll make up de fire."

So we went over to where the canoe was, and while he built a fire in a grassy open place amongst the trees, I fetched meal and bacon and coffee, and coffee-pot and frying-pan, and sugar and tin cups, and the nigger was set back con-

siderable, because he reckoned it was all done with witch-
craft. I catched a good big catfish, too, and Jim cleaned him
with his knife, and fried him.

When breakfast was ready we lolled on the grass and eat
it smoking hot. Jim laid it in with all his might, for he was
most about starved. Then when we had got pretty well
stuffed, we laid off and lazied.

By and by Jim says:

"But looky here, Huck, who wuz it dat 'uz killed in dat
shanty ef it warn't you?"

Then I told him the whole thing, and he said it was smart.
He said Tom Sawyer couldn't get up no better plan that what
I had. Then I says:

"How do you come to be here, Jim, and how'd you get
here?"

He looked pretty uneasy, and didn't say nothing for a minute. Then he says:

"Maybe I better not tell."

"Why, Jim?"

"Well, dey's reasons. But you wouldn' tell on me if I 'uz
to tell you, would you, Huck?"

"Blamed if I would, Jim."

"Well, I b'lieve you, Huck. I—I *run off.*"

"Jim!"

"But mind, you said you wouldn' tell—you know you said
you wouldn' tell, Huck."

"Well, I did. I said I wouldn't, and I'll stick to it. Honest
injun, I will. People would call me a low-down Abolitionist
and despise me for keeping mum—but that don't make no
difference. I ain't a-going to tell, and I ain't a-going back
there, anyways. So, now, le's know all about it."

"Well, you see, it 'uz dis way. Ole missus—dat's Miss Watson—she pecks on me all de time, en treats me pooty rough,

but she alwuz said she wouldn' sell me down to Orleans. But I noticed dey wuz a nigger trader roun' de place considable lately, en I begin to git oneasy. Well, one night I creeps to de do' pooty late, en de do warn't quite shet, en I hear old missus tell de widder she gwyne to sell me down to Orleans, but she didn' want to, but she could git eight hund'd dollars for me, en it 'uz sich a big stack o' money she couldn' resis'. De widder she try to git her to say she wouldn't do it, but I never waited to hear de res'. I lit out mighty quick, I tell you.

"I tuck out en shin down de hill, en 'spec to steal a skift 'long de sho' som'ers 'bove de town, but dey wuz people a-stirring yit, so I hid in de ole tumbledown cooper shop on de bank to wait for everybody to go 'way. Well, I wuz dah all night. Dey wuz somebody roun' all de time. 'Long 'bout six in de mawnin' skifts begin to go by, en 'bout eight er nine every skift dat went 'long wuz talkin' 'bout how yo' pap come over to de town en say you's killed. Dese las' skifts wuz full o' ladies en genlmen a-goin' over for to see de place. Sometimes dey'd pull up at de sho' en take a res' b'for' dey started acrost, so by de talk I got to know all 'bout de killin'. I 'uz powerful sorry you's killed, Huck, but I ain't no mo' now.

"I laid dah under de shavin's all day. I 'uz hungry, but I warn't afeard; bekase I knowed ole missus en de widder wuz goin' to start to de camp-meet'n' right arter breakfas' en be gone all day, en dey knows I goes off wid de cattle 'bout daylight, so dey wouldn' 'spec to see me roun' de place, en so dey wouldn' miss me tell arter dark in de evenin'. De yuther servants wouldn' miss me, kase dey'd shin out en take holiday soon as de ole folks 'uz out'n de way.

"Well, when it come dark I tuck out up de river road, en went 'bout two mile er more to whah dey warn't no houses.

I'd made up my mine 'bout what I's a-gwyne to do. You see, ef I kep' on tryin' to git away afoot, de dogs 'ud track me; ef I stole a skift to cross over, dey'd miss dat skift, you see, en dey'd know 'bout whah I'd lan' on de yuther side, en whah to pick up my track. So I says, a raff is what I's arter; it doan' *make* no track.

"I see a light a-comin' round de p'int bymeby, so I wade' in en shove' a log ahead o' me en swum more'n half-way acrost de river, en got in 'mongst de driftwood, en kep' my head down low, en kinder swum agin de current tell de raff come along. Den I swum to de stern uv it en tuck a-holt. It clouded up en 'uz pooty dark for a little while. So I clumb up en laid down on de planks. De men 'uz all 'way yonder in de middle, whah de lantern wuz. De river wuz a-risin', en dey wuz a good current; so I reck'n'd 'at by fo' in de mawnin' I'd be twenty-five mile down de river, en den I'd slip in jis b'fo' daylight en swim asho', en take to de woods on de Illinois side.

"But I didn' have no luck. When we 'uz mos' down to de head er de islan' a man begin to come aft wid de lantern. I see it warn't no use fer to wait, so I slid overboard en struck out fer de islan'. Well, I had a notion I could lan' mos' any-whers, but I couldn't—bank too bluff. I 'uz mos' to de foot er de islan' b'fo' I foun' a good place. I went into de woods en jedged I wouldn' fool wid raffs no mo', long as dey move de lantern roun' so. I had my pipe en a plug er dog-leg en some matches in my cap, en dey warn't wet, so I wuz all right."

"And so you ain't had no meat nor bread to eat all this time? Why didn't you get mud-turkles?"

"How you gwyne to git 'm? You can't slip up on um en grab um; en how's a body gwyne to hit um wid a rock? How could a body do it in de night? En I warn't gwyne to show myself on de bank in de daytime."

"Well, that's so. You've had to keep in the woods all the

time, of course. Did you hear 'em shooting the cannon?"

"Oh, yes. I knowed dey was arter you. I see um go by heah—watched um thoo de bushes."

Some young birds come along, flying a yard or two at a time and lighting. Jim said it was a sign it was going to rain. He said it was a sign when young chickens flew that way, and so he reckoned it was the same way when young birds done it. I was going to catch some of them, but Jim wouldn't let me. He said it was death. He said his father laid mighty sick once, and some of them catched a bird, and his old granny said his father would die, and he did.

And Jim said you mustn't count the things you are going to cook for dinner, because that would bring bad luck. The same if you shook the table cloth after sundown. And he said if a man owned a beehive and that man died, the bees must be told about it before sun-up next morning, or else the bees would all weaken down and quit work and die. Jim said bees wouldn't sting idiots; but I didn't believe that, because I had tried them lots of times myself, and they wouldn't sting me.

I had heard about some of these things before, but not all of them. Jim knowed all kinds of signs. He said he knowed most everything. I said it looked to me like all the signs was about bad luck, and so I asked him if there warn't any good-luck signs. He says:

"Mighty few—an' *dey* ain't no use to a body. What you want to know when good luck's a-comin' for? Want to keep it off?" And he said: "Ef you's got hairy arms en a hairy breas', it's a sign dat you's a-gwyne to be rich. Well, dey's some use in a sign like dat, 'kase it's so fur ahead. You see, maybe you's got to be po' a long time fust, en so you might git discourage' en kill yo'sef 'f you didn't know by de sign dat you gwyne to be rich bymeby."

"Have you got hairy arms and a hairy breast, Jim?"

"What's de use to ax dat question? Don't you see I has?"

"Well, are you rich?"

"No, but I ben rich wunst, and gwyne to be rich ag'in. Wunst I had foteen dollars, but I tuck to specalat'n, en got busted out."

"What did you speculate in, Jim?"

"Well, fust I tackled stock."

"What kind of stock?"

"Why, live stock—cattle, you know. I put ten dollars in a cow. But I ain' gwyne to resk no mo' money in stock. De cow up 'n' died on my han's."

"So you lost the ten dollars."

"No, I didn't lose it all. I on'y los' 'bout nine of it. I sole de hide en taller for a dollar en ten cents."

"You had five dollars and ten cents left. Did you speculate any more?"

"Yes. You know that one-laigged nigger dat b'longs to old Misto Bradish? Well, he sot up a bank, en say any-body dat put in a dollar would git fo' dollars mo' at de en' er de year. Well, all de niggers went in, but dey didn't have much. I wuz de on'y one dat had much. So I stuck out for mo' dan fo' dollars, en I said 'f I didn' git it I'd start a bank mysef. Well, o' course dat nigger want' to keep me out er de business, bekase he says dey warn't business 'nough for two banks, so he say I could put in my five dollars en he pay me thirty-five at de en' er de year.

"So I done it. Den I reck'n'd I'd inves' de thirty-five dollars right off en keep things a-movin'. Dey wuz a nigger name' Bob, dat had ketched a wood-flat, en his marster didn't know it; en I bought it off'n him en told him to take de thirty-five dollars when de en' er de year come; but some-body stole de wood-flat dat night, en nex' day de one-laigged nigger say de bank's busted. So dey didn' none uv us git no money."

"What did you do with the ten cents, Jim?"

"Well, I 'uz gwyne to spen' it, but I had a dream, en de dream tole me to give it to a nigger name' Balum—Balum's Ass dey call him for short; he's one er dem chuckleheads, you know. But he's lucky, dey say, en I see I warn't lucky. De dream say let Balum inves' de ten cents en he'd make a raise for me. Well, Balum he tuck de money, en when he wuz in church he hear de preacher say dat whoever give to de po' len' to de Lord, en boun' to git his money back a hund'd times. So Balum he tuck en give de ten cents to de po', en laid low to see what wuz gwyne to come of it."

"Well, what did come of it, Jim?"

"Nuffn never come of it. I couldn' manage to k'leck dat money no way; en Balum he couldn'. I ain' gwyne to len' no mo' money 'dout I see de security. Boun' to git yo' money back a hund'd times, de preacher says! Ef I could git de ten *cents* back, I'd call it squah, en be glad er de chanst."

"Well, it's all right anyway, Jim, long as you're going to be rich again some time or other."

"Yes; en I's rich now, come to look at it. I owns mysef, en I's wuth eight hund'd dollars. I wisht I had de money, I wouldn' want no mor."

CHAPTER IX

THE HOUSE OF DEATH FLOATS BY

I WANTED TO go and look at a place right about the middle of the island that I'd found when I was exploring; so we started and soon got to it, because the island was only three miles long and a quarter wide.

This place was a tolerable long, steep hill or ridge about forty foot high. We had a rough time getting to the top, the sides were so steep and the bushes so thick. We tramped and clumb around all over it, and by and by found a good big cavern in the rock, most up to the top on the side towards Illinois. The cavern was as big as two or three rooms bunched together, and Jim could stand up straight in it. It was cool in there. Jim was for putting our traps in there right away, but I said we didn't want to be climbing up and down all the time.

Jim said if we had the canoe hid in a good place, and had all the traps in the cavern, we could rush there if anybody was to come to the island, and they would never find us without dogs. And, besides, he said them little birds had said it was going to rain, and did I want the things to get wet?

So we went back and got the canoe, and paddled up abreast the cavern, and lugged all the traps up there. Then we hunted up a place close by to hide the canoe in, amongst the thick willows. We took some fish off of the lines and set them again, and begun to get ready for dinner.

The door of the cavern was big enough to roll a hogshead in, and on one side of the door the floor stuck out a little bit, and was flat and a good place to build a fire on. So we built it there and cooked dinner.

We spread the blankets inside for a carpet, and ate our dinner in there. We put all the other things handy at the back of the cavern. Pretty soon it darkened up, and begun to thunder and lighten; so the birds was right about it. Directly it begun to rain, and it rained like all fury, too, and I never see the wind blow so. It was one of these regular summer storms. It would get so dark that it looked all blue-black outside, and lovely; and the rain would thrash along by so thick that the trees off a little ways looked dim and spider-webby; and here would come a blast of wind that would bend the trees down and turn up the pale underside of the leaves; and then a perfect ripper of a gust would follow along and set the branches to tossing their arms as if they was just wild; and next, when it was just about the bluest and blackest—*fst!* it was as bright as glory, and you'd have a little glimpse of tree-tops a-plunging about away off yonder in the storm, hundreds of yards further than you could see before; dark as sin again in a second, and now you'd hear the thunder let go with an awful crash, and then go rumbling, grumbling, tumbling, down the sky towards the under side of the world, like rolling empty barrels down-stairs—where it's long stairs and they bounce a good deal, you know.

"Jim, this is nice," I says. "I wouldn't want to be nowhere else but here. Pass me along another hunk of fish and some hot corn-bread."

"Well, you wouldn't 'a' ben here 'f it hadn't 'a' ben for Jim. You'd 'a' ben down dah in de woods widout any dinner, en gittin' mos' drownded, too; dat you would, honey. Chickens knows when it's gwyne to rain, en so do the birds, chile."

The river went on raising and raising for ten or twelve days, till at last it was over the banks. The water was three or four foot deep on the island in the low places and on the Illinois bottom. On that side it was a good many miles wide, but on the Missouri side it was the same old distance

across—a half a mile—because the Missouri shore was just a
wall of high bluffs.

Daytimes we paddled all over the island in the canoe. It
was mighty cool and shady in the deep woods, even if the
sun was blazing outside. We went winding in and out
amongst the trees, and sometimes the vines hung so thick
we had to back away and go some other way. Well, on
every old broken-down tree you could see rabbits and snakes
and such things; and when the island had been overflowed a
day or two they got so tame, on account of being hungry, that
you could paddle right up and put your hand on them if you
wanted to; but not the snakes and turtles—they would slide
off in the water. The ridge our cavern was in was full of
them. We could 'a' had pets enough if we'd wanted them.

One night we catched a little section of a lumber-raft—
nice pine planks. It was twelve foot wide and about
fifteen or sixteen foot long, and the top stood above water
six or seven inches—a solid, level floor.

Another night when we was up at the head of the island,
just before daylight, here comes a frame-house down, on the
west side. She was a two-story, and tilted over considerable.
We paddled out and got aboard—clumb in at an upstairs window. But it was too dark to see yet, so we made
the canoe fast and set in her to wait for daylight.

The light begun to come before we got to the foot of the
island. Then we looked in at the window. We could make
out a bed, and a table, and two old chairs, and lots of things
around about on the floor, and there was clothes hanging
against the wall. There was something laying on the floor in
the far corner that looked like a man. So Jim says:

"Hello, you!"

It didn't budge. So I hollered again, and Jim says:
"De man ain't asleep—he's dead. You hold still."

He went, and bent down and looked, and says:

"It's a dead man. Yes, indeedy; naked, too. He's ben shot in de back. I reck'n he's ben dead two er three days. Come in, Huck, but doan' look at his face—it's too gashly."

I didn't look at him at all. Jim throwed some old rags over him but he needn't done it; I didn't want to see him. There was heaps of old greasy cards scattered around over the floor, and old whisky-bottles, and a couple of masks made out of blackcloth; and all over the walls was the ignorantest kind of words and pictures made with charcoal. There was two old dirty calico dresses, and a sun-bonnet, and some women's underclothes hanging against the wall, and some men's clothing, too. We put the lot into the canoe —it might come good. There was a boy's old speckled straw hat on the floor; I took that, too. And there was a bottle that had had milk in it, and it had a rag stopper for a baby to suck. We would 'a' took the bottle, but it was broke. There was a seedy old chest, and an old hair trunk with the hinges broke. They stood open, but there warn't nothing left in them that was any account. The way things was scattered about we reckoned the people left in a hurry, and warn't fixed so as to carry off most of their stuff.

We got an old tin lantern, and a butcher-knife without any handle, and a bran-new Barlow knife worth two bits in any store, and a lot of tallow candles, and a tin candle-stick, and a gourd, and a tin cup, and a ratty old bedquilt off the bed, and a reticule with needles and pins and beeswax and buttons and thread and all such truck in it, and a hatchet and some nails, and a fish-line as thick as my little finger with some monstrous hooks on it, and a roll of buck-skin, and a leather dog-collar, and a horseshoe, and some vials of medicine that didn't have no label on them; and just as we was leaving I found a tolerable good currycomb, and Jim he found a ratty old fiddle-bow, and a wooden leg. The straps was broke off of it, but, barring that, it was a good enough leg, though it was too long for me and not long enough for Jim, and we couldn't find the other one.

And so, take it all around, we made a good haul. When we was ready to shove off we was a quarter of a mile below the island, and it was pretty broad day; so I made Jim lay down in the canoe and cover up with the quilt, because if he set up people could tell he was a nigger a good ways off. I paddled over to the Illinois shore, and drifted down most a half a mile doing it. I crept up the dead water under the bank, and hadn't no accidents and didn't see nobody. We got home all safe.

CHAPTER X

WHAT COMES OF HANDLIN' SNAKE-SKIN

AFTER BREAKFAST I wanted to talk about the dead man and guess out how he come to be killed, but Jim didn't want to. He said it would fetch bad luck; and besides, he said, he might come and ha'nt us; he said a man that warn't buried was more likely to go a-ha'nting around than one that was planted and comfortable. That sounded pretty reasonable, so I didn't say no more; but I couldn't keep from studying over it and wishing I knowed who shot the man, and what they done it for.

We rummaged the clothes we'd got, and found eight dollars in silver sewed up in the lining of an old blanket overcoat. Jim said he reckoned the people in that house stole the coat, because if they'd 'a' knowed the money was there they wouldn't 'a' left it. I said I reckoned they killed him, too; but Jim didn't want to talk about that. I says:

"Now you think it's bad luck; but what did you say when I fetched in the snake-skin that I found on the top of the ridge day before yesterday? You said it was the worst bad luck in the world to touch a snake-skin with my hands. Well, here's your bad luck! We've raked in all this truck and eight dollars besides. I wish we could have some bad luck like this every day, Jim."

"Never you mind, honey, never you mind. Don't you git too peart. It's a-comin'. Mind I tell you it's a-comin'."

It did come, too. It was a Tuesday that we had that talk. Well, after dinner Friday we was laying around in the grass at the upper end of the ridge, and got out of tobacco. I went to the cavern to get some, and found a rattlesnake in there. I killed him, and curled him up on the foot of Jim's blanket, ever so natural, thinking there'd be some fun when Jim found him there. Well, by night I forgot all about the snake, and when Jim flung himself down on the blanket while I struck a light the snake's mate was there, and bit him.

He jumped up yelling, and the first thing the light showed was the varmint curled up and ready for another spring. I laid him out in a second with a stick, and Jim grabbed pap's whisky-jug and begun to pour it down.

He was barefooted, and the snake bit him right on the heel. That all comes of my being such a fool as to not remember that wherever you leave a dead snake its mate always comes there and curls around it. Jim told me to chop off the snake's head and throw it away, and then skin the body and roast a piece of it. I done it, and he eat it and said it would help cure him. He made me take off the rattles and tie them around his wrist, too. He said that that would help. Then I slid out quiet and throwed the snakes clear away amongst the bushes; for I warn't going to let Jim find out it was all my fault, not if I could help it.

Jim sucked and sucked at the jug, and now and then he got out of his head and pitched around and yelled; but every time he come to himself he went to sucking at the jug again. His foot swelled up pretty big, and so did his leg; but by and by the drunk begun to come, and so I judged he was all right; but I'd druther been bit with a snake than pap's whisky.

Jim was laid up for four days and nights. Then the swelling was all gone and he was around again. I made up my mind I wouldn't ever take a-holt of a snake-skin again with my hands, now that I see what had come of it. Jim said he reckoned I would believe him next time. And he said that handling a snake-skin was such awful bad luck that maybe we hadn't got to the end of it yet. He said he druther see the new moon over his left shoulder as much as a thousand times than take up a snake-skin in his hand. Well, I was getting to feel that way myself, though I've always reckoned that looking at the new moon over your left shoulder is one of the carelessest and foolishest things a body can do. Old Hank Bunker done it once, and bragged about it; and in less than two years he got drunk and fell off of the shot-tower, and spread himself out so that he was just a kind of a layer, as you may say; and they slid him edgeways between two barn doors for a coffin, and buried him so, so they say, but I didn't see it. Pap told me. But anyway it all come of looking at the moon that way, like a fool.

Well, the days went along, and the river went down between its banks again; and about the first thing we done was to bait one of the big hooks with a skinned rabbit and set it and catch a catfish that was as big as a man, being six foot two inches long, and weighed over two hundred pounds. We couldn't handle him, of course; he would 'a' flung us into Illinois. We just set there and watched him rip and tear around till he drownded. We found a brass button in his stomach and a round ball, and lots of rubbage. We split the ball open with the hatchet, and there was a spool in it. Jim said he'd had it there a long time, to coat it over so and make a ball of it. It was as big a fish as was ever catched in the Mississippi, I reckon. Jim said he hadn't ever seen a bigger one. He would 'a' been worth a good deal over at the village. They peddle out such a fish as that by the pound in the market-house there; everybody buys some of him; his meat's as white as snow and makes a good fry.

Next morning I said it was getting slow and dull, and I wanted to get a stirring-up some way. I said I reckoned I would slip over the river and find out what was going on. Jim liked that notion; but he said I must go in the dark, and look sharp. Then he studied it over and said, couldn't I put on some of them old things and dress up like a girl? That was a good notion, too. So we shortened up one of the calico gowns, and I turned up my trouser-legs to my knees and got into it. Jim hitched it behind with the hooks, and it was a fair fit. I put on the sun-bonnet and tied it under my chin, and then for a body to look in and see my face was like looking down a joint of stove-pipe. Jim said nobody would know me, even in the daytime, hardly. I practised around all day to get the hang of the things, and by and by I could do pretty well in them, only Jim said I didn't walk like a girl; and he said I must quit pulling up my gown to get at my britches-pocket. I took notice, and done better.

I started up the Illinois shore in the canoe just after dark.

I started across to the town from a little below the ferry-landing, and the drift of the current fetched me in at the bottom of the town. I tied up and started along the bank. There was a light burning in a little shanty that hadn't been lived in for a long time, and I wondered who had took up quarters there. I slipped up and peeped in at the window. There was a woman about forty year old in there knitting by a candle that was on a pine table. I didn't know her face; she was a stranger, for you couldn't start a face in that town that I didn't know. Now this was lucky, because I was weakening; I was getting afraid I had come; people might know my voice and find me out. But if this woman had been in such a little town two days she could tell me all I wanted to know; so I knocked at the door, and made up my mind I wouldn't forget I was a girl.

CHAPTER XI

THEY'RE AFTER US!

"COME IN," says the woman, and I did. She says: "Take a cheer."

I done it. She looked me all over with her little shiny eyes, and says:

"What might your name be?"

"Sarah Williams."

"Where'bouts do you live? In this neighborhood?"

"No'm. In Hookerville, seven mile below. I've walked all the way and I'm all tired out."

"Hungry, too, I reckon. I'll find you something."

"No'm, I ain't hungry. I was so hungry I had to stop two miles below here at a farm; so I ain't hungry no more. It's what make me so late. My mother's down sick, and out of money and everything, and I come to tell my uncle Abner Moore. He lives at the upper end of the town, she says. I hain't ever been here before. Do you know him?"

"No; but I don't know everybody yet. I haven't lived here quite two weeks. It's a considerable ways to the upper end of the town. You better stay here all night. Take off your bonnet."

"No," I says; "I'll rest awhile, I reckon, and go on. I ain't afeard of the dark."

She said she wouldn't let me go by myself, but her husband would be in by and by, maybe in a hour and a half, and she'd send him along with me. Then she got to talking about her husband, and about her relations up the river, and her relations down the river, and about how much better off they used to was, and how they didn't know but they'd made a mistake coming to our town, instead of letting well alone—and so on and so on, till I was afeared I had made a mistake coming to her to find out what was going on in the town; but by and by she dropped on to pap and the murder, and then I was pretty willing to let her clatter right along. She told about me and Tom Sawyer finding the twelve thousand dollars (only she got it twenty) and all about pap and what a hard lot he was, and what a hard lot I was, and at last she got down to where I was murdered. I says:

"Who done it? We've heard considerable about these goings-on down in Hookerville, but we don't know who 'twas that killed Huck Finn."

"Well, I reckon there's a right smart chance of people *here* that 'd like to know who killed him. Some think old Finn done it himself."

"No—is that so?"

"Most everybody thought it at first. He'll never know how nigh he come to getting lynched. But before night they changed around and judged it was done by a runaway nigger named Jim."

"Why *he*—"

I stopped. I reckoned I better keep still. She run on, and never noticed I had put in at all:

"The nigger run off the very night Huck Finn was killed. So there's a reward out for him—three hundred dollars. And there's a reward out for old Finn, too—two hundred dollars. You see, he come to town the morning after the murder, and told about it, and was out with 'em on the ferry-boat hunt, and right away after he up and left. Before night they wanted to lynch him, but he was gone, you see. Well, next day they found out the nigger was gone; they found out he hadn't been seen sence ten o'clock the night the murder was done. So then they put it on him, you see; and while they was full of it, next day, back comes old Finn, and went boo-hooing to Judge Thatcher to get money to hunt for the nigger all over Illinois with. The judge gave him some, and that evening he got drunk, and was around till after midnight with a couple of mighty hard-looking strangers, and then went off with them. Well, he hain't come back sence, and they ain't looking for him back till this thing blows over a little, for people thinks now that he killed his boy and fixed things so folks would think robbers done it, and then he'd get Huck's money without having to bother a long time with a lawsuit. People do say he warn't any too good to do it. Oh, he's sly, I reckon. If he don't come back for a year he'll be all right. You can't prove anything on him, you know; everything will be quieted down then, and he'll walk in Huck's money as easy as nothing."

"Yes, I reckon so, 'm. I don't see nothing in the way of it. Has everybody quit thinking the nigger done it?"

"Oh, no, not everybody. A good many thinks he done it. But they'll get the nigger pretty soon now, and maybe they can scare it out of him."

"Why, are they after him yet?"

"Well, you're innocent, ain't you! Does three hundred dollars lay around every day for people to pick up? Some folks think the nigger ain't far from here. I'm one of them—but I hain't talked it around. A few days ago I was talking with an old couple that lives next door in the log shanty, and they happened to say hardly anybody ever goes to that island over yonder that they call Jackson's Island. Don't anybody live there? says I. No, nobody, says they. I didn't say any more, but I done some thinking. I was pretty near certain I'd seen smoke over there, about the head of the island, a day or two before that, so I says to myself, like as not that nigger's hiding over there; anyway, says I, it's worth the trouble to give the place a hunt. I hain't seen any smoke sence, so I reckon maybe he's gone, if it was him; but my husband's going over to see—him and another man. He was gone up the river; but he got back to-day, and I told him as soon as he got here two hours ago."

I had got so uneasy I couldn't set still. I had to do something with my hands; so I took up a needle off of the table and went to threading it. My hands shook, and I was making a bad job of it. When the woman stopped talking I looked up, and she was looking at me pretty curious and smiling a little. I put down the needle and thread, and let on to be interested—and I was, too—and says:

"Three hundred dollars is a power of money. I wish my mother could get it. Is your husband going over there to-night?"

"Oh, yes. He went up-town with the man I was telling you of, to get a boat and see if they could borrow another gun. They'll go over after midnight."

"Couldn't they see better if they was to wait till daytime?"

"Yes. And couldn't the nigger see better, too? After midnight he'll likely be asleep, and they can slip around through the woods and hunt up his campfire all the better for the dark, if he's got one."

"I didn't think of that."

The woman kept looking at me pretty curious, and I didn't feel a bit comfortable. Pretty soon she says:

"What did you say your name was, honey?"

"M—Mary Williams."

Somehow it didn't seem to me that I said it was Mary before, so I didn't look up—seemed to me I said Sarah; so I felt sort of cornered, and was afeard maybe I was looking it, too. I wished the woman would say something more; the longer she set still the uneasier I was. But now she says:

"Honey, I thought you said it was Sarah when you first come in?"

"Oh, yes'm, I did. Sarah Mary Williams. Sarah's my first name. Some calls me Sarah, some calls me Mary."

"Oh, that's the way of it?"

"Yes'm."

I was feeling better then, but I wished I was out of there, anyway. I couldn't look up yet.

Well, the woman fell to talking about how hard times was, and how poor they had to live, and how the rats was as free as if they owned the place, and so forth and so on, and then I got easy again. She was right about the rats. You'd see one stick his nose out of a hole in the corner every little while. She said she had to have things handy to throw at them when she was alone, or they wouldn't give her no peace. She showed me a bar of lead twisted up into a knot, and said she was a good shot with it generly, but she'd wrenched her arm a day or two ago, and didn't know whether she could throw true now. But she watched for a chance, and directly banged away at a rat; but she missed him wide, and said, "Ouch!" it hurt her arm so. Then she told me to try for the next one. I wanted to be getting away before the old man got back, but of course I didn't let on. I got the thing, and the first rat that showed his nose I let drive, and if he'd 'a' stayed where he was he'd 'a' been a tolerable sick rat. She said that was first-rate, and she reckoned I would hive the next one. She went and got the lump of lead and fetched it back, and brought along a hank of yarn which she wanted me to help her with. I held up my two hands and she put the hank over them, went on talking about her and her husband's matters. But she broke off to say:

"Keep your eye on the rats. You better have the lead in your lap, handy."

So she dropped the lump into my lap just as that moment,

and I clapped my legs together on it and she went on talking. But only about a minute. Then she took off the hank and looked me straight in the face, and very pleasant, and says:

"Come, now, what's your real name?"

"Wh-hat, mum?"

"What's your real name? Is it Bill, or Tom, or Bob?—or what is it?"

I reckon I shook like a leaf, and I didn't know hardly what to do. But I says:

"Please to don't poke fun at a poor girl like me, mum. If I'm in the way here, I'll—"

"No, you won't. Set down and stay where you are. I ain't going to hurt you, and I ain't going to tell on you, nuther. You just tell me your secret, and trust me. I'll keep it; and, what's more, I'll help you. So'll my old man if you want him to. You see, you're a runaway 'prentice, that's all. It ain't anything. There ain't no harm in it. You've been treated bad, and you made up your mind to cut. Bless you, child, I wouldn't tell on you. Tell me all about it now, that's a good boy."

So I said it wouldn't be no use to try to play it any longer, and I would just make a clean breast and tell her everything, but she mustn't go back on her promise. Then I told her my father and mother was dead, and the law had bound me out to a mean farmer in the country thirty mile back from the river, and he treated me so bad I couldn't stand it no longer; he went away to be gone a couple of days, and so I took my chance and stole some of his daughter's old clothes and cleared out, and I had been three nights coming the thirty miles. I traveled nights, and hid daytimes and slept, and the bag of bread and meat I carried from home lasted me all the way, and I had a-plenty. I said I believed my uncle

Abner Moore would take care of me, and so that was why I struck out for this town of Goshen.

"Goshen, child? This ain't Goshen. This is St. Petersburg. Goshen's ten mile further up the river. Who told you this was Goshen?"

"Why, a man I met at daybreak this morning, just as I was going to turn into the woods for my regular sleep. He told me when the roads forked I must take the right hand, and five mile would fetch me to Goshen."

"He was drunk, I reckon. He told you just exactly wrong."

"Well, he did act like he was drunk, but it ain't no matter now. I got to be moving along. I'll fetch Goshen before daylight."

"Hold on a minute. I'll put you up a snack to eat. You might want it."

So she put me up a snack, and says:

"Say, when a cow's laying down, which end of her gets up first? Answer up prompt now—don't stop to study over it. Which end gets up first?"

"The hind end, mum."

"Well, then a horse?"

"The for'rard end, mum."

"Which side of a tree does the moss grow on?"

"North side."

"If fifteen cows is browsing on a hillside, how many of them eats with their heads pointed the same direction?"

"The whole fifteen, mum."

"Well, I reckon you *have* lived in the country. I thought maybe you was trying to hocus me again. What's your real name, now?"

"George Peters, mum."

"Well, try to remember it, George. Don't forget and tell me it's Elexander before you go, and then get out by saying it's George Elexander when I catch you. And don't go about women in that old calico. You do a girl tolerable poor, but you might fool men, maybe. Bless you, child, when you set out to thread a needle don't hold the thread still and fetch the needle up to it; hold the needle still and poke the thread at it; that's the way a woman most always does, but a man always does t'other way. And when you throw at a rat or anything, hitch yourself up a-tiptoe and fetch your hand up over your head as awkward as you can, and miss your rat about six or seven foot. Throw stiff-armed from the shoulder, like there was a pivot there for it to turn on, like a girl; not from the wrist and elbow, with your arm out to one side, like a boy. And, mind you, when a girl tries to catch anything in her lap she throws her knees apart; she don't clap them together, the way you did when you catched the lump of lead. Why, I spotted you for a boy when you was threading the needle; and I contrived the other things just to make certain. Now trot along to your uncle, Sarah Mary William George Elexander Peters, and if you get into trouble you send word to Mrs. Judith Loftus, which is me, and I'll do what I can to get you out of it. Keep the river road all the way, and next time you tramp take shoes and socks with you. The river road's a rocky one, and your feet'll be in a condition when you get to Goshen, I reckon."

I went up the bank about fifty yards, and then I doubled on my tracks and slipped back to where my canoe was, a good piece below the house. I jumped in, and was off in a hurry. I went up-stream far enough to make the head of the island, and then started across. I took off the sun-bonnet, for I didn't want no blinders on then. When I was about the middle I heard the clock begin to strike, so I stops and listens; the sound come faint over the water but clear— eleven. When I struck the head of the island I never waited to blow, though I was most winded, but I shoved right into the timber where my old camp used to be, and started a good fire there on a high and dry spot.

Then I jumped in the canoe and dug out for our place, a mile and a half below, as hard as I could go. I landed, and slopped through the timber and up the ridge and into the cavern. There Jim laid, sound asleep on the ground. I roused him out and says:

"Git up and hump yourself, Jim! There ain't a minute to lose. They're after us!"

Jim never asked no questions, he never said a word; but the way he worked for the next half an hour showed about how he was scared. By that time everything we had in the world was on our raft, and she was ready to be shoved out from the willow cove where she was hid. We put out the camp-fire at the cavern the first thing, and didn't show a candle outside after that.

I took the canoe out from the shore a little piece, and took a look; but if there was a boat around I couldn't see it, for stars and shadows ain't good to see by. Then we got out the raft and slipped along down in the shade, past the foot of the island dead still—never saying a word.

CHAPTER XII

"BETTER LET BLAME WELL ALONE"

IT MUST 'A' been close on to one o'clock when we got
below the island at last, and the raft did seem to go mighty
slow. If a boat was to come along we was going to take
to the canoe and break for the Illinois shore; and it was well
a boat didn't come, for we hadn't ever thought to put the
gun in the canoe, or a fishing-line, or anything to eat. We
was in ruther too much of a sweat to think of so many
things. It warn't good judgment to put *everything* on the raft.

If the men went to the island I just expect they found the
camp-fire I built, and watched it all night for Jim to come.
Anyways, they stayed away from us, and if my building the
fire never fooled them it warn't no fault of mine. I played it
as low down on them as I could.

When the first streak of day began to show we tied up to a
towhead in a big bend on the Illinois side, and hacked off
cottonwood branches with the hatchet, and covered up the
raft with them so she looked like there had been a cave-in in
the bank there. A towhead is a sand-bar with cottonwoods
on it thick as harrow-teeth.

We had mountains on the Missouri shore and heavy
timber on the Illinois side, and the channel was down the
Missouri shore at that place, so we warn't afraid of anybody
running across us. We laid there all day, and watched the
rafts and steamboats spin down the Missouri shore, and up-
bound steamboats fight the big river in the middle. I told
Jim all about the time I had jabbering with that woman; and
Jim said she was a smart one, and if she was to start after us

106

herself *she* wouldn't set down and watch a camp-fire—no, sir, she'd fetch a dog. Well, then, I said, why couldn't she tell her husband to fetch a dog? Jim said he bet she did think of it by the time the men was ready to start and he believed they must 'a' gone up-town to get a dog and so they lost all that time, or else we wouldn't be here on a towhead sixteen or seventeen mile below the village—no, indeedy, we would be in that same old town again. So I said I didn't care what was the reason they didn't get us as long as they didn't.

When it was beginning to come on dark we poked our heads out of the cottonwood thicket, and looked up and down and across; nothing in sight; so Jim took up some of the top planks of the raft and built a snug wigwam to get under in blazing weather and rainy, and to keep the things dry. Jim made a floor for the wigwam, and raised it a foot or more above the level of the raft, so now the blankets and all the traps was out of reach of steamboat waves. Right in the middle of the wigwam we made a layer of dirt about five or six inches deep with a frame around it for to hold it to its place, this was to build a fire on in sloppy weather or chilly; the wigwam would keep it from being seen. We made an extra steering-oar, too, because one of the others might get broke on a snag or something. We fixed up a short forked stick to hang the old lantern on, because we must always light the lantern whenever we see a steamboat coming down-stream, to keep from getting run over; but we wouldn't have to light it for upstream boats unless we see we was in what they call a "crossing"; for the river was pretty high yet, very low banks being still a little under water; so up-bound boats didn't always run the channel, but hunted easy water.

This second night we run between seven and eight hours, with a current that was making over four mile an hour. We

catched fish and talked, and we took a swim now and then
to keep off sleepiness. It was kind of solemn, drifting down
the big, still river, laying on our backs looking up at the stars,
and we didn't even feel like talking loud, and it warn't
often that we laughed—only a little kind of a low chuckle.
We had mighty good weather as a general thing, and
nothing ever happened to us at all—that night, nor the next,
nor the next.

Every night we passed towns, some of them away up on
black hillsides, nothing but just a shiny bed of lights; not a
house could you see. The fifth night we passed St. Louis, and
it was like the whole world lit up. In St. Petersburg they used
to say there was twenty or thirty thousand people in St. Louis,
but I never believed it till I see that wonderful spread of
lights at two o'clock that still night. There warn't a sound
there; everybody was asleep.

Every night now I used to slip ashore toward ten o'clock
at some little village, and buy ten or fifteen cents' worth of
meal or bacon or other stuff to eat; and sometimes I lifted a
chicken that warn't roosting comfortable, and took him
along. Pap always said, take a chicken when you get a
chance, because if you don't want him yourself you can
easy find somebody that does, and a good deed ain't ever
forgot, but I never see pap when he didn't want the chicken
himself.

Mornings before daylight I slipped into corn-fields and
borrowed a watermelon, or a mushmelon, or a punkin, or
some new corn, or things of that kind. Pap always said it
warn't no harm to borrow things if you was meaning to pay
them back some time; but the widow said it warn't anything
but a soft name for stealing, and no decent body would do it.
Jim said he reckoned the widow was partly right and pap
was partly right; so the best way would be for us to pick out

two or three things from the list and say we wouldn't borrow them any more—then he reckoned it wouldn't be no harm to borrow the others. So we talked it over all one night, drifting along down the river, trying to make up our minds whether to drop the watermelons, or the cantelopes, or the mushmelons, or what. But toward daylight we got it all settled satisfactory, and concluded to drop crab apples and p'simmons. We warn't feeling just right before that, but it was all comfortable now. I was glad the way it come out, too, because crab apples ain't ever good, and the p'simmons wouldn't be ripe for two or three months yet.

We shot a water-fowl now and then that got up too early in the morning or didn't go to bed early enough in the evening. Take it all round, we lived pretty high.

The fifth night below St. Louis we had a big storm after midnight, with a power of thunder and lightning, and the rain poured down in a solid sheet. We stayed in the wigwam and let the raft take care of itself. When the lightning glared out we could see a big straight river ahead, and high, rocky bluffs on both sides. By and by says I "Hel-*lo*, Jim, looky yonder!" It was a steamboat that had killed herself on a rock. We was drifting straight down for her. The lightning showed her very distinct. She was leaning over, with part of her upper deck above water, and you could see every little chimbly-guy clean and clear, and a chair by the big bell, with an old slouch hat hanging on the back of it, when the flashes come.

Well, it being away in the night and stormy, and all so mysterious-like, I felt just the way any other boy would 'a' felt when I seen that wreck laying there so mournful and lonesome in the middle of the river. I wanted to get aboard of her and slink around a little, and see what there was there. So I says:

"Le's land on her, Jim."

But Jim was dead against it at first. He says:

"I doan' want to go fool'n 'long er no wrack. We's doin' blame' well, en we better let blame' well alone, as de good book says. Like as not dey's a watchman."

"Watchman your grandmother," I says; "there ain't nothing to watch but the texas and the pilot-house; and do you reckon anybody's going to resk his life for a texas and a pilot-house such a night as this, when it's likely to break up and wash off down the river any minute?" Jim couldn't say nothing to that, so he didn't try. "And besides," I says, "we might borrow something worth having out of the captain's stateroom. Seegars, *I* bet you—and cost five cents apiece, solid cash. Steamboat captains is always rich, and get sixty dollars a month, and *they* don't care a cent what a thing costs, you know, long as they want it. Stick a candle in your pocket; I can't rest, Jim, till we give her a rummaging. Do you reckon Tom Sawyer would ever go by this thing? Not for pie, he wouldn't. He'd call it an adventure—that's what he'd call it; and he'd land on that wreck if it was his last act. And wouldn't he throw style into it?—wouldn't he spread himself, nor nothing?"

Jim he grumbled a little, but give in. He said we mustn't talk any more than we could help, and then talk mighty low. The lightning showed us the wreck again just in time, and we fetched the stabboard derrick, and made fast there.

The deck was high out here. We went sneaking down the slope of it to labboard, in the dark, towards the texas, feeling our way slow with our feet, and spreading our hands out to fend off the guys, for it was so dark we couldn't see no sign of them. Pretty soon we struck the forward end of the skylight, and clumb on to it; and the next step fetched us in front of the captain's door, which was open, and by Jimminy, away down through the texas-hall we see a light! and all in the same second we seem to hear low voices in yonder!

Jim whispered and said he was feeling powerful sick, and told me to come along. I says, all right, and was going to start for the raft; but just then I heard a voice wail out and say:

"Oh, please don't, boys; I swear I won't ever tell!"

Another voice said, pretty loud:

"It's a lie, Jim Turner. You've acted this way before. You always want more'n your share of the truck, and you've always got it, too, because you've swore 't if you didn't you'd tell. But this time you've said it jest one time too many. You're the meanest, treacherousest hound in this country."

By this time Jim was gone for the raft. I was just a-biling with curiosity; and I says to myself, Tom Sawyer wouldn't back out now, and so I won't either; I'm a-going to see what's going on here. So I dropped on my hands and knees in the little passage, and crept aft in the dark till there warn't but one stateroom betwixt me and the cross-hall of the texas. Then in there I see a man stretched on the floor and tied hand and foot, and two men standing over him, and one of them had a dim lantern in his hand, the other one had a pistol. This one kept pointing the pistol at the man's head on the floor, and saying:

"I'd *like* to! And I orter, too—a mean skunk!"

The man on the floor would shrivel up and say, "Oh, please don't, Bill; I hain't ever goin' to tell."

And every time he said that the man with the lantern would laugh and say:

" 'Deed you *ain't!* You never said no truer thing 'n that, you bet you." And once he said: "Hear him beg! and yit if we hadn't got the best of him and tied him he'd 'a' killed us both. And what *for?* Jist for noth'n'. Jist because we stood on our *rights*—that's what for. But I lay you ain't a-goin' to threaten nobody any more, Jim Turner. Put *up* that pistol, Bill."

Bill says:

"I don't want to, Jake Packard. I'm for killin' him—and didn't he kill old Hatfield jist the same way—and don't he deserve it?"

"But I don't *want* him killed, and I've got my reasons."

"Bless yo' heart for them words, Jake Packard! I'll never forget you long's I live!" says the man on the floor, sort of blubbering.

Packard didn't take no notice of that, but hung up his lantern on a nail and started toward where I was, there in the dark, and motioned Bill to come. I crawfished as fast as I could about two yards, but the boat slanted so that I couldn't make very good time; so to keep from getting run over and catched I crawled into a stateroom on the upper side. The man came a-pawing along in the dark, and when Packard got to my stateroom, he says:

"Here—come in here."

And in he come, and Bill after him. But before they got in I was up in the upper berth, cornered, and sorry I come. Then they stood there, with their hands on the ledge of the berth, and talked. I couldn't see them, but I could tell where they was by the whisky they'd been having. I was glad I didn't drink whisky; but it wouldn't made much difference anyway, because most of the time they couldn't 'a' treed me because I didn't breathe. I was too scared. And, besides, a body *couldn't* breathe and hear such talk. They talked low and earnest. Bill wanted to kill Turner. He says:

"He's said he'll tell, and he will. If we was to give both our shares to him *now* it wouldn't make no difference after the row and the way we've served him. Shore's you're born, he'll turn state's evidence; now you hear *me*. I'm for putting him out of his troubles."

"So'm I," says Packard, very quiet.

"Blame it, I'd sorter begun to think you wasn't. Well, then, that's all right. Le's go and do it."

"Hold on a minute; I hain't had my say yit. You listen to me. Shooting's good, but there's quieter ways if the thing's *got* to be done. But what *I* say is this: it ain't good sense to go court'n around after a halter if you can git at what you're up to in some way that's jist as good and at the same time don't bring you into no resks. Ain't that so?"

"You bet it is. But how you goin' to manage it this time?"

"Well, my idea is this: we'll rustle around and gather up whatever pickin's we've overlooked in the staterooms, and shove for shore and hide the truck. Then we'll wait. Now I say it ain't a-goin' to be more'n two hours befo' this wrack breaks up and washes off down the river. See? He'll be drownded, and won't have nobody to blame for it but his own self. I reckon that's a considerable sight better 'n killin' of him. I'm unfavorable to killin' a man as long as you can git aroun' it; it ain't good sense, it ain't good morals. Ain't I right?"

"Yes, I reck'n you are. But s'pose she *don't* break up and wash off?"

"Well, we can wait the two hours anyway and see, can't we?"

"All right, then; come along."

So they started, and I lit out, all in a cold sweat, and scrambled forward. It was dark as pitch there; but I said, in a kind of a coarse whisper, "Jim!" and he answered up, right at my elbow, with a sort of moan, and I says:

"Quick, Jim, it ain't no time for fooling around and moaning; there's a gang of murderers in yonder, and if we don't hunt up their boat and set her drifting down the river so these fellow's can't get away from the wreck there's one of 'em going to be in a bad fix. But if we find their boat we car put *all* of 'em in a bad fix—for the sheriff 'll get 'em. Quick—hurry! I'll hunt the labboard side, you hunt the stabboard. You start at the raft, and—"

"Oh, my lordy, lordy! *Raf'?* Dey ain' no raf' no mo'; she done broke loose en gone!—en here we is!"

CHAPTER XIII

HONEST LOOT FROM THE "WALTER SCOTT"

WELL, I CATCHED my breath and most fainted. Shut up on a wreck with such a gang as that! But it warn't no time to be sentimentering. We'd *got* to find that boat now—had to have it for ourselves. So we went a-quaking and shaking down the stabboard side, and slow work it was, too—seemed a week before we got to the stern. No sign of a boat. Jim said he didn't believe he could go any farther—so scared he hadn't hardly any strength left, he said. But I said, come on, if we get left on this wreck we are in a fix, sure. So on we prowled again. We struck for the stern of the texas, and found it, and then scrabbled along forwards on the skylight, hanging on from shutter to shutter, for the edge of the skylight was in the water. When we got pretty close to the cross-hall door there was the skiff, sure enough! I could just barely see her. I felt ever so thankful. In another second I would 'a' been aboard of her, but just then the door opened. One of the men stuck his head out only about a couple of foot from me, and I thought I was gone; but he jerked it in again, and says:

"Heave that blame lantern out o' sight, Bill!"

He flung a bag of something into the boat, and then got in himself and set down. It was Packard. Then Bill *he* come out and go in. Packard says, in a low voice:

"All ready—shove off!"

I couldn't hardly hang on to the shutters, I was so weak. But Bill says:

"Hold on—'d you go through him?"

"No. Didn't you?"

"No. So he's got his share o' the cash yet."

"Well, then, come along; no use to take truck and leave money."

"Say, won't he suspicion what we're up to?"

"Maybe he won't. But we got to have it anyway. Come along."

So they got out and went in.

The door slammed to because it was on the careened side; and in a half second I was in the boat, and Jim come tumbling after me. I out with my knife and cut the rope, and away we went!

We didn't touch an oar, and we didn't speak nor whisper, nor hardly even breathe. We went gliding swift along, dead silent, past the tip of the paddle-box, and past the stern; then in a second or two more we was a hundred yards below the wreck, and the darkness soaked her up, every last sign of her, and we was safe, and knowed it.

When we was three or four hundred yards downstream we see the lantern show like a little spark at the texas door for a second, and we knowed by that that the rascals had missed their boat, and was beginning to understand that they was in just as much trouble now as Jim Turner was.

Then Jim manned the oars, and we took out after our raft. Now was the first time that I begun to worry about the men—I reckon I hadn't had time to before. I begun to think how dreadful it was, even for murderers, to be in such a fix. I says to myself, there ain't no telling but I might come to be a murderer myself yet, and then how would I like it? So says I to Jim:

"The first light we see we'll land a hundred yards below it or above it, in a place where it's a good hiding-place for you and the skiff, and then I'll go and fix up some kind of a yarn, and get somebody to go for that gang and get them out of their scrape, so they can be hung when their time comes."

But that idea was a failure; for pretty soon it begun to storm again, and this time worse than ever. The rain poured down, and never a light showed; everybody in bed, I reckon. We boomed along down the river, watching for lights, and watching for our raft. After a long time the rain let up, but the clouds stayed, and the lightning kept whimpering, and by and by a flash showed us a black thing ahead, floating and we made for it.

It was the raft, and mighty glad was we to get aboard of it again. We seen a light now away down to the right, on shore. So I said I would go for it. The skiff was half full of plunder which that gang had stole there on the wreck. We hustled it on to the raft in a pile, and I told Jim to float along down, and show a light when he judged he had gone about two mile, and keep it burning till I come; and then I manned my oars and shoved for the light. As I got down towards it three or four more showed—up on a hillside. It was a village. I closed in above the shore light, and laid on my oars and floated. As I went by I see it was a lantern hanging on the jackstaff of a double-hull ferryboat. I skimmed around for the watchman, a-wondering whereabouts he slept; and by and by I found him roosting on the bitts forward, with his head down between his knees. I gave his shoulder two or three little shoves, and begun to cry.

He stirred up in a kind of a startlish way; but when he see it was only me he took a good gap and stretch, and then he says:

"Hello, what's up? Don't cry, bub. What's the trouble?"

I says:

"Pap, and mam, and sis, and—"

Then I broke down. He says:

"Oh, dang it now, *don't* take on so; we all has to have our

troubles, and this 'n 'll come out all right. What's the matter
with 'em?"

"They're—they're—are you the watchman of the boat?"

"Yes," he says, kind of pretty-well-satisfied like. "I'm the
captain and the owner and the mate and the pilot and
watchman and head deck-hand; and sometimes I'm the
freight and passengers. I ain't as rich as old Jim Hornback,
and I can't be so blame' generous and good to Tom, Dick,
and Harry as what he is, and slam around money the way he
does; but I've said many a time 't I wouldn't trade places
with him; for, says I, a sailor's life's the life for me, and I'm
derned if *I'd* live two mile out o' town, where there ain't
nothing ever goin' on, not for all his spondulicks and as
much more on top of it. Says I—"

I broke in and says:

"They're in an awful peck of trouble, and—"

"*Who* is?"

"Why, pap and mam and sis and Miss Hooker; and if you'd
take your ferry boat and go up there—"

"Up where? Where are they?"

"On the wreck."

"What wreck?"

"Why, there ain't but one."

"What, you don't mean the *Walter Scott?*"

"Yes."

"Good land! what are they doin' *there,* for gracious
sakes?"

"Well, they didn't go there a-purpose."

"I bet they didn't! Why, great goodness, there ain't no
chance for 'em if they don't git off mighty quick! Why, how
in the nation did they ever git into such a scrape?"

"Easy enough. Miss Hooker was a-visiting up there to the
town—"

"Yes, Booth's Landing—go on."

"She was a-visiting there at Booth's Landing, and just in the edge of the evening she started over with her nigger woman in the horse-ferry to stay all night at her friend's house, Miss What-you-may-call-her—I disremember her name—and they lost their steering-oar, and swung around and went a-floating down, stern first, about two mile, and saddle-baggsed on the wreck, and the ferryman and the nigger woman and the horses was all lost, but Miss Hooker she made a grab and got aboard the wreck. Well, about an hour after dark we come along down in our trading-scow, and it was so dark we didn't notice the wreck till we was right on it; and so *we* saddle-baggsed; but all of us was saved but Bill Whipple—and oh, he *was* the best cretur!—I most wish 't it had been me, I do."

"My George! It's the beatenest thing I ever struck. And *then* what did you all do?"

"Well, we hollered and took on, but it's so wide there we couldn't make nobody hear. So pap said somebody got to get ashore and get help somehow. I was the only one that could swim, so I made a dash for it, and Miss Hooker she said if I didn't strike help sooner, come here and hunt up her uncle, and he'd fix the thing. I made the land about a mile below, and been fooling along ever since, trying to get people to do something, but they said, 'What, in such a night and such a current? There ain't no sense in it; go for the steam-ferry.' Now if you'll go and—"

"By Jackson, I'd *like* to, and, blame it, I don't know but I will; but who in the dingnation's a-going to *pay* for it? Do you reckon your pap—"

"Why *that's* all right. Miss Hooker she tole me, *particular,* that her uncle Hornback—"

"Great guns! is *he* her uncle? Looky here, you break for that light over yonder-way, and turn out west when you git there, and about a quarter of a mile out you'll come to the tavern; tell 'em to dart you out to Jim Hornback's, and he'll foot the bill. And don't you fool around any, because he'll want to know the news. Tell him I'll have his niece all safe before he can get to town. Hump yourself, now; I'm a-going up around the corner here to roust out my engineer."

I struck for the light, but as soon as he turned the corner I went back and got into my skiff and bailed her out, and then pulled up shore in the easy water about six hundred yards, and tucked myself in among some wood-boats; for I couldn't rest easy till I could see the ferryboat start. But take it all around, I was feeling ruther comfortable on accounts of taking all this trouble for that gang, for not many would 'a' done it. I wished the widow knowed about it. I judged she would be proud of me for helping these rapscallions, because rapscallions and dead-beats is the kind the widow and good people takes the most interest in.

Well, before long here comes the wreck, dim and dusky, sliding along down! A kind of cold shiver went through me, and then I struck out for her. She was very deep, and I see in a minute there warn't much chance for anybody being alive in her. I pulled all around her and hollered a little, but there wasn't any answer; all dead still. I felt a little bit heavy-hearted about the gang, but not much, for I reckoned if they could stand it I could.

Then here comes the ferryboat; so I shoved for the middle of the river on a long down-stream slant; and when I judged I was out of eye-reach I laid on my oars, and looked back and see her go and smell around the wreck for Miss Hooker's remainders, because the captain would know her uncle Hornback would want them; and then pretty soon the ferryboat give it up and went for the shore, and I laid into my work and went a-booming down the river.

It did seem a powerful long time before Jim's light showed

up; and when it did show it looked like it was a thousand
mile off. By the time I got there the sky was beginning to get
a little gray in the east; so we struck for an island, and hid
the raft, and sunk the skiff, and turned in and slept like
dead people.

CHAPTER XIV

WAS SOLOMON WISE?

BY AND BY, when we got up, we turned over the truck the gang had stole off of the wreck, and found boots, and blankets, clothes, and all sorts of other things, and a lot of books, and a spy-glass, and three boxes of seegars. We hadn't ever been this rich before in neither of our lives. The seegars was prime. We laid off all the afternoon in the woods talking, and me reading the books, and having a general good time. I told Jim all about what happened inside the wreck and at the ferryboat, and I said these kinds of things was adventures; but he said he didn't want no more adventures. He said that when I went in the texas and he crawled back to get on the raft and found her gone he nearly died, because he judged it was all up with *him* anyway it could be fixed; for if he didn't get saved he would get drownded; and if he did get saved, whoever saved him would send him back home so as to get the reward, and then Miss Watson would sell him South, sure. Well, he was right; he was most always right; he had an uncommon level head for a nigger.

I read considerable to Jim about kings and dukes and earls and such, and how gaudy they dressed, and how much style they put on, and called each other your majesty, and your grace, and your lordship, and so on, 'stead of mister; and Jim's eyes bugged out, and he was interested. He says:

"I didn't know dey was so many un um. I hain't hearn 'bout none un um, skasely, but ole King Sollermun, onless you counts dem kings dat's in a pack er k'yards. How much do a king git?"

"Get?" I says; "why, they get a thousand dollars a month if they want it; they can have just as much as they want; everything belongs to them."

"*Ain'* dat gay? En what dey got to do, Huck?"

"*They* don't do nothing! Why, how you talk! They just set around."

"No; is dat so?"

"Of course it is. They just set around—except, maybe, when there's a war; then they go to the war. But other times they just lazy around; or go hawking—just hawking and sp— Sh!—d'you hear a noise?"

We skipped out and looked; but it warn't nothing but the flutter of a steamboat's wheel away down, coming around the point; so we come back.

"Yes," says I, "and other times, when things is dull, they fuss with the parlyment; and if everybody don't go just so he whacks their heads off. But mostly they hang round the harem."

"Roun' de which?"

"Harem."

"What's de harem?"

"The place where he keeps his wives. Don't you know about the harem? Solomon had one; he had about a million wives."

"Why, yes, dat's so; I—I'd done forgot it. A harem's a bo'd'n-house, I reck'n. Mos' likely dey has rackety times in de nussery. En I reck'n de wives quarrels considable; en dat 'crease de racket. Yit dey say Sollermun de wises' man dat ever live'. I doan' take no stock in dat. Bekase why: would a wise man want to live in de mids' er sich a blim-blammin' all de time? No—'deed he wouldn't. A wise man 'ud take en buil' a biler-factry; en den he could shet *down* de biler-factry when he want to res'."

"Well, but he *was* the wisest man, anyway; because the widow she told me so, her own self."

"I doan' k'yer what de widder say, he *warn't* no wise man nuther. He had some er de dad-fetchedes' ways I ever see. Does you know 'bout dat chile dat he 'uz gwyne to chop in two?"

"Yes, the widow told me all about it."

"*Well,* den! Warn' dat de beatenes' notion in de worl'? You jes' take en look at it a minute. Dah's de stump, dah— dat's one er de women; heah's you—dat's de yuther one; I's Sollermun; en dish yer dollar bill's de chile. Bofe un you claims it. What does I do? Does I shin aroun' mongs' de neighbors en fine out which un you de bill *do* b'long to, en han' it over to de right one, all safe en soun', de way dat anybody dat had any gumption would? No; I take en whack de bill in *two,* en give half un it to you, en de yuther half to de yuther woman. Dat's de way Sollermun was gwyne to do wid de chile. Now I want to ast you: what's de use er dat half a bill?—can't buy noth'n wid it. En what use is half a chile? I wouldn' give a dern for a million un um."

"But hang it, Jim, you've clean missed the point—blame it, you've missed it a thousand mile."

"Who? Me? Go 'long. Doan' talk to *me* 'bout yo' pints. I reck'n I knows sense when I sees it; en dey ain' no sense in sich doin's as dat. De 'spute warn't 'bout a half a chile, de 'spute was 'bout a whole chile; en de man dat think he kin settle a 'spute 'bout a whole chile wid a half a chile doan' know enough to come in out'n de rain. Doan' talk to me 'bout Sollermun, Huck, I knows him by de back."

"But I tell you you don't get the point."

"Blame de pint! I reck'n I knows what I knows. En mine you, de *real* pint is down furder—it's down deeper. It lays in de way Sollermun was raised. You take a man dat's

got on'y one or two chillen; is dat man gwyne to be waseful
o' chillen? No, he ain't; he can't 'ford it. *He* know how to
value 'em. But you take a man dat's got 'bout five million
chillen runnin' roun' de house, en it's diffunt. *He* as soon chop
a chile in two as a cat. Dey's plenty mo'. A chile er two, mo'
er less, warn't no consekens to Sollermun, dad fetch him!"

I never see such a nigger. If he got a notion in his head
once, there warn't no getting it out again. He was the most
down on Solomon of any nigger I ever see. So I went to
talking about other kings, and let Solomon slide. I told
about Louis Sixteenth that got his head cut off in France long
time ago; and about his little boy the dolphin, that would 'a'
been a king, but they took and shut him up in jail, and some
say he died there.

"Po' little chap."

"But some says he got out and away, and come to
America."

"Dat's good! But he'll be pooty lonesome—dey ain' no
kings here, is dey, Huck?"

"No."

"Den he cain't git no situation. What he gwyne to do?"

"Well, I don't know. Some of them gets on the police, and
some of them learns people how to talk French."

"Why, Huck, doan' de French people talk de same way we
does?"

"*No,* Jim; you couldn't understand a word they said—not
a single word."

"Well, now, I be ding-busted! How do dat come?"

"*I* don't know; but it's so. I got some of their jabber out of
a book. S'pose a man was to come to you and say Polly-
voo-franzy—what would you think?"

"I wouldn' think nuffn; I'd take en bust him over de head
—dat is, if he warn't white. I wouldn't 'low no nigger to call
me dat."

"Shucks, it ain't calling you anything. It's only saying, do you know how to talk French?"

"Well, den, why couldn't he say it?"

"Why, he *is* a-saying it. That's a Frenchman's *way* of saying it."

"Well, it's a blame ridicklous way, en I doan' want to hear no mo' 'bout it. Dey ain' no sense in it."

"Looky here, Jim; does a cat talk like we do?"

"No, a cat don't."

"Well, does a cow?"

"No, a cow don't nuther."

"Does a cat talk like a cow, or a cow talk like a cat?"

"No, dey don't."

"It's natural and right for 'em to talk different from each other, ain't it?"

"Course."

"And ain't it natural and right for a cat and a cow to talk different from *us?*"

"Why, mos' sholy it is."

"Well, then, why ain't it natural and right for a *Frenchman* to talk different from us? You answer me that."

"Is a cat a man, Huck?"

"No."

"Well, den, dey ain't no sense in a cat talkin' like a man. Is a cow a man?—er is a cow a cat?"

"No, she ain't either of them."

"Well, den, she ain't got no business to talk like either one er the yuther of 'em. Is a Frenchman a man?"

"Yes."

"Well, den! Dad blame it, why doan' he *talk* like a man? You answer me *dat!"*

I see it warn't no use wasting words—you can't learn a nigger to argue. So I quit.

CHAPTER XV

FOOLING POOR OLD JIM

WE JUDGED that three nights more would fetch us to Cairo, at the bottom of Illinois, where the Ohio River comes in, and that was what we was after. We would sell the raft and get on a steamboat and go way up the Ohio amongst the free states, and then be out of trouble.

Well, the second night a fog begun to come on, and we made for a towhead to tie to, for it wouldn't do to try to run in a fog; but when I paddled ahead in the canoe, with the line to make fast, there warn't anything but little saplings to tie to. I passed the line around one of them right on the edge of the cut bank, but there was a stiff current, and the raft come booming down so lively she tore it out by the roots and away she went. I see the fog closing down, and it made me so sick and scared I couldn't budge for most a half a minute it seemed to me—and then there warn't no raft in sight; you couldn't see twenty yards. I jumped into the canoe and run back to the stern, and grabbed the paddle and set her back a stroke. But she didn't come. I was in such a hurry I hadn't untied her. I got up and tried to untie her, but I was so excited my hands shook so I couldn't hardly do anything with them.

As soon as I got started I took out after the raft, hot and heavy, right down the towhead. That was all right as far as it went, but the towhead warn't sixty yards long, and the minute I flew by the foot of it I shot out into the solid white fog, and hadn't no more idea which way I was going than a dead man.

Thinks I, it won't do to paddle; first I know I'll run into the bank or a towhead or something; I got to set still and float, and yet it's mighty fidgety business to have to hold your hands still at such a time. I whooped and listened. Away down there somewheres I hears a small whoop, and up comes my spirits. I went tearing after it, listening sharp to hear it again. The next time it come I see I warn't heading for it, but heading away to the right of it. And the next time I was heading away to the left of it—and not gaining on it much either, for I was flying around, this way and that and t'other, but it was going straight ahead all the time.

I did wish the fool would think to beat a tin pan, and beat it all the time, but he never did, and it was the still places between the whoops that was making the trouble for me. Well, I fought along, and directly I hears the whoop *behind* me. I was tangled good now. That was somebody else's whoop, or else I was turned around.

I throwed the paddle down. I heard the whoop again; it was behind me yet, but in a different place; it kept coming, and kept changing its place, and I kept answering, till by and by it was in front of me again, and I knowed the current had swung the canoe's head downstream, and I was all right if that was Jim and not some other raftsman hollering. I couldn't tell nothing about voices in a fog, for nothing don't look natural nor sound natural in a fog.

The whooping went on, and in about a minute I come a-booming down on a cut bank with smoky ghosts of big trees on it, and the current throwed me off to the left and shot by, amongst a lot of snags that fairly roared, the current was tearing by them so swift.

In another second or two it was solid white and still again. I set perfectly still then, listening to my heart thump, and I reckon I didn't draw a breath while it thumped a hundred.

I just give up then. I knowed what the matter was. That cut bank was an island, and Jim had gone down t'other side of it. It warn't no towhead that you could float by in ten minutes. It had the big timber of a regular island; it might be five or six miles long and more than half a mile wide.

I kept quiet, with my ears cocked, about fifteen minutes, I reckon. I was floating along, of course, four or five miles an hour; but you don't ever think of that. No, you *feel* like you are laying dead still on the water; and if a little glimpse of a snag slips by you don't think to yourself how fast *you're* going, but you catch your breath and think, my! how that snag's tearing along. If you think it ain't dismal and lonesome out in a fog that way by yourself in the night, you try it once —you'll see.

Next, for about a half an hour, I whoops now and then; at last I hears the answer a long ways off, and tries to follow it, but I couldn't do it, and directly I judged I'd got into a nest of towheads, for I had little dim glimpses of them on both sides of me—sometimes just a narrow channel between, and some that I couldn't see I knowed was there because I'd hear the wash of the current against the old dead brush and trash that hung over the banks. Well, I warn't long loosing the whoops down amongst the towheads; and I only tried to chase them a little while, anyway, because it was worse than chasing a Jack-o'-lantern. You never knowed a sound dodge around so, and swap places so quick and so much.

I had to claw away from the bank pretty lively four or five times, to keep from knocking the islands out of the river; and so I judged the raft must be butting into the bank every now and then, or else it would get further ahead and clear out of hearing—it was floating a little faster than what I was.

Well, I seemed to be in the open river again by and by, but

I couldn't hear no sign of a whoop nowheres. I reckoned Jim had fetched up on a snag, maybe, and it was all up with him. I was good and tired, so I laid down in the canoe and said I wouldn't bother no more. I didn't want to go to sleep, of course; but I was so sleepy I couldn't help it; so I thought I would take jest one little cat-nap.

But I reckon it was more than a cat-nap, for when I waked up the stars was shining bright, the fog was all gone, and I was spinning down a big bend stern first. First I didn't know where I was; I thought I was dreaming; and when things began to come back to me they seemed to come up dim out of last week.

It was a monstrous big river here, with the tallest and the thickest kind of timber on both banks; just a solid wall, as well as I could see by the stars. I looked away down-stream, and seen a black speck on the water. I took after it; but when I got to it it warn't nothing but a couple of saw-logs made fast together. Then I see another speck, and chased that; then another, and this time I was right. It was the raft.

When I got to it Jim was setting there with his head down between his knees, asleep, with his right arm hanging over the steering-oar. The other oar was smashed off, and the raft was littered up with leaves and branches and dirt. So she'd had a rough time.

I made fast and laid down under Jim's nose on the raft and began to gap, and stretch my fists out against Jim, and says:

"Hello, Jim, have I been asleep? Why didn't you stir me up?"

"Goodness gracious, is dat you, Huck? En you ain' dead—you ain' drownded—you's back ag'in? It's too good for true, honey, it's too good for true. Lemme look at you chile, lemme feel o' you. No, you ain' dead! you's back ag'in, 'live

en soun', jis de same ole Huck—de same ole Huck, thanks to goodness!"

"What's the matter with you, Jim? You been a-drinking?"

"Drinkin'? Has I ben a-drinkin'? Has I had a chance to be a-drinkin'?"

"Well, then, what makes you talk so wild?"

"How does I talk wild?"

"How? Why, hain't you been talking about my coming back, and all that stuff, as if I'd been gone away?"

"Huck—Huck Finn, you look me in de eye; look me in de eye. *Hain't* you ben gone away?"

"Gone away? Why, what in the nation do you mean? *I* hain't been gone anywheres. Where would I go to?"

"Well, looky here, boss, dey's sumfn wrong, dey is. Is I *me,* or who *is* I? Is I heah, or whah *is* I? Now dat's what I wants to know."

"Well, I think you're here, plain enough, but I think you're a tangle-headed old fool, Jim."

"I is, is I? Well, you answer me dis: Didn't you tote out de line in de canoe fer to make fas' to de towhead?"

"No, I didn't. What towhead? I hain't seen no towhead."

"You hain't seen no towhead? Looky here, didn't de line pull loose en de raf' go a-hummin' down de river, en leave you en de canoe behine in de fog?"

"What fog?"

"Why, *de* fog!—de fog dat's been aroun' all night. En didn't you whoop, en didn't I whoop, tell we got mix' up in de islands en one un us got los' en t'other one was jis' as good as los', 'kase he didn' know whah he wuz? En didn't I bust up agin a lot er dem islands en have a turrible time en mos' git drownded? Now ain' dat so, boss—ain't it so? You answer me dat."

"Well, this is too many for me, Jim. I hain't seen no fog,

nor no islands, nor no troubles, nor nothing. I been setting
here talking with you all night till you went to sleep about ten
minutes ago, and I reckon I done the same. You couldn't
'a' got drunk in that time, so of course you've been dreaming."

"Dad fetch it, how is I gwyne to dream all dat in ten
minutes?"

"Well, hang it all, you did dream it, because there didn't
any of it happen."

"But, Huck, it's all jis' as plain to me as—"

"It don't make no difference how plain it is; there ain't
nothing in it. I know, because I've been here all the time."

Jim didn't say nothing for about five minutes, but set
there studying over it. Then he says:

"Well, den, I reck'n I did dream it, Huck; but dog my
cats ef it ain't de powerfulest dream I ever see. En I hain't
ever had no dream b'fo' dat's tired me like dis one."

"Oh, well, that's all right, because a dream does tire a body
like everything sometimes. But this one was a staving dream;
tell me all about it, Jim."

So Jim went to work and told me the whole thing right
through, just as it happened, only he painted it up considerable. Then he said he must start in and " 'terpret" it,
because it was sent for a warning. He said the first towhead
stood for a man that would try to do us some good, but the
current was another man that would get us away from him.
The whoops was warnings that would come to us every now
and then, and if we didn't try hard to make out to understand them they'd just take us into bad luck, 'stead of keeping us out of it. The lot of towheads was troubles we was
going to get into with quarrelsome people and all kinds of
mean folks, but if we minded our business and didn't talk
back and aggravate them, we would pull through and get

out of the fog and into the big clear river, which was the free states, and wouldn't have no more trouble.

It had clouded up pretty dark just after I got on to the raft, but it was clearing up again now.

"Oh, well, that's all interpreted well enough as far as it goes, Jim," I says; "but what does *these* things stand for?"

It was the leaves and rubbish on the raft and the smashed oar. You could see them first-rate now.

Jim looked at the trash, and then looked at me, and back at the trash again. He had got the dream fixed so strong in his head that he couldn't seem to shake it loose and get the facts back into its place again right away. But when he did get the thing straightened around he looked at me steady without ever smiling, and says:

"What do dey stan' for? I's gwyne to tell you. When I got all wore out wid work, en wid de callin' for you, en went to sleep, my heart wuz mos' broke bekase you wuz los', en I didn' k'yer no' mo' what become er me en de raf'. En when I wake up en fine you back ag'in, all safe en soun', de tears come, en I could 'a' got down on my knees en kiss yo' foot, I's so thankful. En all you wuz thinkin' 'bout wuz how you could make a fool uv ole Jim wid a lie. Dat truck dah is *trash;* en trash is what people is dat puts dirt on de head er dey fren's en makes 'em ashamed."

Then he got up slow and walked to the wigwam, and went in there without saying anything but that. But that was enough. It made me feel so mean I could almost kissed *his* foot to get him to take it back.

It was fifteen minutes before I could work myself up to go and humble myself to a nigger; but I done it, and I warn't ever sorry for it afterward, neither. I didn't do him no more mean tricks, and I wouldn't done that one if I'd 'a' knowed it would make him feel that way.

CHAPTER XVI

THE RATTLESNAKE-SKIN DOES ITS WORK

WE SLEPT MOST all day, and started out at night, a little ways behind a monstrous long raft that was as long going by as a procession. She had four long sweeps at each end, so we judged she carried as many as thirty men, likely. She had five big wigwams aboard, wide apart, and an open camp-fire in the middle, and a tall flag-pole at each end. There was a power of style about her. It *amounted* to something being a raftsman on such a craft as that.

We went drifting down into a big bend, and the night clouded up and got hot. The river was very wide, and was walled with solid timber on both sides; you couldn't see a break in it hardly ever, or a light. We talked about Cairo, and wondered whether we would know it when we got to it. I said likely we wouldn't, because I had heard say there warn't but about a dozen houses there, and if they didn't happen to have them lit up, how was we going to know we was passing a town? Jim said if the two big rivers joined together there, that would show. But I said maybe we might think we was passing the foot of an island and coming into the same old river again. That disturbed Jim—and me too. So the question was, what to do? I said, paddle ashore the first time a light showed, and tell them pap was behind, coming along with a trading-scow, and was a green hand at the business, and wanted to know how far it was to Cairo. Jim thought it was a good idea, so we took a smoke on it and waited.

There warn't nothing to do now but to look out sharp for

the town, and not pass it without seeing it. He said he'd be mighty sure to see it, because he'd be a free man the minute he seen it, but if he missed it he'd be in a slave country again and no more show for freedom.

Every little while he jumps up and says:

"Dah she is?"

But it warn't. It was Jack-o'-lanterns, or lightning-bugs; so he set down again, and went to watching, same as before. Jim said it made him all over trembly and feverish to be so close to freedom. Well, I can tell you it made me all over trembly and feverish, too, to hear him, because I began to get it through my head that he *was* most free—and who was to blame for it? Why, *me*. I couldn't get that out of my conscience, no how nor no way. It got to troubling me so I couldn't rest; I couldn't stay still in one place. It hadn't ever come home to me before, what this thing was that I was doing. But now it did; and it stayed with me, and scorched me more and more. I tried to make out to myself that *I* warn't to blame, because *I* didn't run Jim off from his rightful owner; but it warn't no use, conscience up and says, every time, "But you knowed he was running for his freedom, and you could 'a' paddled ashore and told somebody." That was so—I couldn't get around that no way. That was where it pinched. Conscience says to me, "What had poor Miss Watson done to you that you could see her nigger go off right under your eyes and never say one single word? What did that poor old woman do to you that you could treat her so mean? Why, she tried to learn you your book, she tried to learn you your manners, she tried to be good to you every way she knowed how. *That's* what she done."

I got to feeling so mean and miserable I most wished I was dead. I fidgeted up and down the raft, abusing myself to myself, and Jim was fidgeting up and down past me. We neither of us could keep still. Every time he danced around and says, "Dah's Cairo!" it went through me like a shot, and I thought if it *was* Cairo I reckoned I would die of miserableness.

Jim talked out loud all the time while I was talking to myself. He was saying how the first thing he would do when he got to a free state he would go to saving up money and never spend a single cent, and when he got enough he would buy his wife, which was owned on a farm close to where Miss Watson lived; and then they would both work to buy the two children, and if their master wouldn't sell them, they'd get an Ab'litionist to go and steal them.

It most froze me to hear such talk. He wouldn't ever dared to talk such talk in his life before. Just see what a difference it made in him the minute he judged he was about free. It was according to the old saying "Give a nigger an inch and he'll take an ell." Thinks I, this is what comes of my not thinking. Here was this nigger, which I had as good as helped to run away, coming right out flat-footed and saying he would steal his children—children that belonged to a man I didn't even know; a man that hadn't ever done me no harm.

I was sorry to hear Jim say that, it was such a lowering of him. My conscience got to stirring me up hotter than ever, until at last I says to it, "Let up on me—it ain't too late yet—I'll paddle ashore at the first light and tell." I felt easy and happy and light as a feather right off. All my troubles was gone. I went to looking out sharp for a light, and sort of singing to myself. By and by one showed. Jim sings out:

"We's safe, Huck, we's safe! Jump up and crack yo' heels! Dat's de good ole Cairo at las', I jis knows it!"

I says:

"I'll take the canoe and go and see, Jim. It mightn't be, you know."

He jumped and got the canoe ready, and put his old coat in the bottom for me to set on, and give me the paddle; and as I shoved off, he says:

"Pooty soon I'll be a-shout'n' for joy, en I'll say, it's all on accounts o' Huck; I's a free man, en I couldn't ever been free ef it hadn' ben for Huck; Huck done it. Jim won't ever forgit you, Huck; you's de bes' fren' Jim's ever had; en you's de *only* fren' ole Jim's got now."

I was paddling off, all in a sweat to tell on him; but when he says this, it seemed to kind of take the tuck all out of me. I went along slow then, and I warn't right down certain whether I was glad I started or whether I warn't. When I was fifty yards off, Jim says:

"Dah you goes, de old true Huck; de on'y white genlman dat ever kep' his promise to old Jim."

Well, I just felt sick. But I says, I *got* to do it—I can't get *out* of it. Right then along comes a skiff with two men in it with guns, and they stopped and I stopped. One of them says:

"What's that yonder?"

"A piece of a raft," I says.

"Do you belong on it?"

"Yes, sir."

"Any men on it?"

"Only one, sir."

"Well, there's five niggers run off to-night up yonder, above the head of the bend. Is your man white or black?"

I didn't answer up prompt. I tried to, but the words wouldn't come. I tried for a second or two to brace up and out with it but I warn't man enough—hadn't the spunk of a rabbit. I see I was weakening; so I just give up trying and up and says:

"He's white."

"I reckon we'll go and see for ourselves."

"I wish you would," says I, "because it's pap that's there, and maybe you'd help me tow the raft ashore where the light is. He's sick—and so is mam and Mary Ann."

"Oh, the devil! we're in a hurry, boy. But I s'pose we've got to. Come, buckle to your paddle, and let's get along."

I buckled to my paddle and they laid to their oars. When we had made a stroke or two, I says:

"Pap 'll be mighty much obleeged to you, I can tell you. Everybody goes away when I want them to help me tow the raft ashore, and I can't do it by myself."

"Well, that's infernal mean. Odd, too. Say, boy, what's the matter with your father?"

"It's the—a—the—well, it ain't anything much."

They stopped pulling. It warn't but a mighty little ways to the raft now. One says:

"Boy, that's a lie. What *is* the matter with your pap? Answer up square now, and it 'll be the better for you."

"I will, sir, I will, honest—but don't leave us, please. It's the—the— Gentlemen, if you'll only pull ahead, and let me heave you the headline, you won't have to come a-near the raft—please do."

"Set her back, John, set her back!" says one. They backed water. "Keep away, boy—keep to looard. Confound it, I just expect the wind has blowed it to us. Your pap's got the smallpox, and you know it precious well. Why didn't you come out and say so? Do you want to spread it all over?"

"Well," says I, a-blubbering, "I've told everybody before, and they just went away and left us."

"Poor devil, there's something in that. We are right down sorry for you, but we—well, hang it, we don't want the small-pox, you see. Look here, I'll tell you what to do. Don't you try to land yourself, or you'll smash everything to pieces. You float down about twenty miles, and you'll come to a

town on the left-hand side of the river. It will be long after
sun-up then, and when you ask for help you tell them your
folks are all down with chills and fever. Don't be a fool again,
and let people guess what is the matter. Now we're trying to
do you a kindness; so you just put twenty miles between us,
that's a good boy. It wouldn't do any good to land yonder
where the light is——it's only a wood-yard. Say, I reckon
your father's poor, and I'm bound to say he's in pretty hard
luck. Here, I'll put a twenty-dollar gold piece on this board,
and you get it when it floats by. I feel mighty mean to leave
you; but my kingdom! it won't do to fool with smallpox,
don't you see?"

"Hold on, Parker," says the man, "here's a twenty to put
on the board for me. Good-by, boy; you do as Mr. Parker
told you, and you'll be all right."

"That's so, my boy—good-by, good-by. If you see any
runaway niggers you get help and nab them, and you can
make some money by it."

"Good-by, sir," says I; "I won't let no runaway niggers get
by me if I can help it."

They went off and I got aboard the raft, feeling bad and
low, because I knowed very well I had done wrong, and I see
it warn't no use for me to try to learn to do right; a body that
don't get *started* right when he's little ain't got no show—
when the pinch comes there ain't nothing to back him up and
keep him to his work, and so he gets beat. Then I thought a
minute, and says to myself, hold on; s'pose you'd 'a' done
right and give Jim up would you felt better than what you do
now? No, says I, I'd feel bad—I'd feel just the same way I do
now. Well, then, says I, what's the use you learning to do
right when it's troublesome to do right and ain't no trouble to
do wrong, and the wages is just the same? I was stuck. I
couldn't answer that. So I reckoned I wouldn't bother no

more about it, but after this always do whichever come handiest at the time.

I went into the wigwam; Jim warn't there. I looked all around; he warn't anywhere. I says:

"Jim!"

"Here I is, Huck. Is dey out o' sight yit? Don't talk loud."

He was in the river under the stern oar, with just his nose out. I told him they were out of sight, so he come aboard. He says:

"I was a-listenin' to all de talk, en I slips into de river en was gwyne to shove for sho' if dey come aboard. Den I was gwyne to swim to de raf' agin when dey was gone. But lawsy, how you did fool 'em, Huck! Dat *wuz* de smartes' dodge! I tell you, chile, I 'spec it save' ole Jim—ole Jim ain't going to forgit you for dat, honey."

Then we talked about the money. It was a pretty good raise—twenty dollars apiece. Jim said we could take deck passage on a steamboat now, and the money would last us as far as we wanted to go in the free states. He said twenty mile more warn't far for the raft to go, but he wished we was already there.

Towards daybreak we tied up, and Jim was mighty particular about hiding the raft good. Then he worked all day fixing things in bundles, and getting all ready to quit rafting.

That night about ten we hove in sight of the lights of a town away down in a left-hand bend.

I went off in the canoe to ask about it. Pretty soon I found a man out in the river with a skiff, setting a trotline. I ranged up and says:

"Mister, is that town Cairo?"

"Cairo? No. You must be a blame' fool."

"What town is it, mister?"

"If you want to know, go and find out. If you stay here botherin' around me for about a half a minute longer you'll get something you won't want."

I paddled to the raft. Jim was awful disappointed, but I said never mind, Cairo would be the next place, I reckoned.

We passed another town before daylight, and I was going out again; but it was high ground, so I didn't go. No high ground about Cairo, Jim said. I had forgot it. We laid up for the day on a towhead tolerable close to the left-hand bank. I begun to suspicion something. So did Jim. I says:

"Maybe we went by Cairo in the fog that night."

He says:

"Doan' le's talk about it, Huck. Po' niggers can't have no luck. I awluz 'spected dat rattlesnake-skin warn't done wid its work."

"I wish I'd never seen that snake-skin, Jim—I do wish I'd never laid eyes on it."

"It ain't yo' fault, Huck; you didn't know. Don't you blame yo'self 'bout it."

When it was daylight, here was the clear Ohio water inshore, sure enough, and outside was the old regular Muddy! So it was all up with Cairo.

We talked it all over. It wouldn't do to take to the shore; we couldn't take the raft up the stream, of course. There warn't no way but to wait for dark, and start back in the canoe and take the chances. So we slept all day amongst the cotton wood thicket, so as to be fresh for the work, and when we went back to the raft about dark the canoe was gone!

We didn't say a word for a good while. There warn't anything to say. We both knowed well enough it was some more work of the rattlesnake-skin; so what was the use to talk about it? It would only look like we was finding fault, and that would be bound to fetch more bad luck—and keep on fetching it, too, till we knowed enough to keep still.

By and by we talked about what we better do, and found there warn't no way but just to go along down with the raft till we got a chance to buy a canoe to go back in. We warn't going to borrow it when there warn't anybody around, the way pap would do, for that might set people after us.

So we shoved out after dark on the raft.

Anybody that don't believe yet that it's foolishness to handle a snake-skin, after all that that snake-skin done for us, will believe it now if they read on and see what more it done for us.

The place to buy canoes is off of rafts laying up at shore. But we didn't see no rafts laying up; so we went along during three hours and more. Well, the night got gray and ruther thick, which is the next meanest thing to fog. You can't tell the shape of the river, and you can't see no distance. It got to be very late and still, and then along comes a steamboat up the river. We lit the lantern, and judged she would see it. Up-stream boats didn't generly come close to us; they go out and follow the bars and hunt for easy water under the reefs; but nights like this they bull right up the channel against the whole river.

We could hear her pounding along, but we didn't see her good till she was close. She aimed right for us. Often they do that and try to see how close they can come without touching; sometimes the wheel bites off a sweep, and then the pilot sticks his head out and laughs, and thinks he's mighty smart. Well, here she comes, and we said she was going to try and shave us; but she didn't seem to be sheering off a bit. She was a big one, and she was coming in a hurry, too, looking like a black cloud with rows of glow-worms around it; but all of a sudden she bulged out, big and scary, with a long row of wide-open furnace doors shining like red-hot teeth, and her monstrous bows and guards hanging right over us. There was a yell at us, and a jingling of bells to stop the engines, a powwow of cussing, and whistling of steam—and as Jim went overboard on one side and I on the other, she come smashing straight through the raft.

I dived—and I aimed to find the bottom, too, for a thirty-foot wheel had got to go over me, and I wanted it to have plenty of room. I could always stay under water a minute; this time I reckon I stayed under a minute and a half. Then I bounced for the top in a hurry, for I was nearly busting. I popped out to my armpits and blowed the water out of my nose and puffed a bit. Of course there was a booming current; and of course that boat started her engines again ten seconds after she stopped them, for they never cared much for raftsmen; so now she was churning along up the river, out of sight in the thick weather, though I could hear her.

I sung out for Jim about a dozen times, but I didn't get any answer; so I grabbed a plank that touched me while I was "treading water," and struck out for shore, shoving it ahead of me. But I made out to see that the drift of the current was towards the left-hand shore, which meant that I was in a crossing; so I changed off and went that way.

It was one of these long, slanting, two-mile crossings; so I was a good long time in getting over. I made a safe landing, and clumb up the bank. I couldn't see but a little ways, but I went poking along over rough ground for a quarter of a mile or more, and then I run across a big old-fashioned double log house before I noticed it. I was going to rush by and get away, but a lot of dogs jumped out and went howling and barking at me, and I knowed better than to move another peg.

CHAPTER XVII

THE GRANGERFORDS TAKE ME IN

IN ABOUT A minute somebody spoke out of a window without putting his head out, and says:

"Be done, boys! Who's there?"

I says:

"It's me."

"Who's me?"

"George Jackson, sir."

"What do you want?"

"I don't want nothing, sir. I only want to go along by, but the dogs won't let me."

"What are you prowling around here this time of night for—hey?"

"I warn't prowling around, sir; I fell overboard off the steamboat."

"Oh, you did, did you? Strike a light there, somebody. What did you say your name was?"

"George Jackson, sir. I'm only a boy."

"Look here, if you're telling the truth you needn't be afraid—nobody 'll hurt you. But don't try to budge; stand right where you are. Rouse out Bob and Tom, some of you, and fetch the guns. George Jackson, is there anybody with you?"

"No, sir, nobody."

I heard the people stirring around in the house now, and see a light. The man sung out:

"Snatch that light away, Betsy, you old fool—ain't you got any sense? Put it on the floor behind the front door. Bob, if you and Tom are ready, take your places."

"All ready."

"Now, George Jackson, do you know the Shepherdsons?"

"No, sir; I never heard of them."

"Well, that may be so, and it mayn't. Now, all ready. Step forward, George Jackson. And mind, don't you hurry—come mighty slow. If there's anybody with you, let him keep back—if he shows himself he'll be shot. Come along now. Come slow; push the door open yourself—just enough to squeeze in, d'you hear?"

I didn't hurry; I couldn't if I'd a-wanted to. I took one slow step at a time and there warn't a sound, only I thought I could hear my heart. The dogs were as still as the humans, but they followed a little behind me. When I got to the three log doorsteps I heard them unlocking and unbarring and unbolting. I put my hand on the door and pushed it a little and a little more till somebody said, "There, that's enough—put your head in." I done it, but I judged they would take it off.

The candle was on the floor, and there they all was, looking at me, and me at them, for about a quarter of a minute: Three big men with guns pointed at me, which made me wince, I tell you; the oldest, gray and about sixty, the other two thirty or more—all of them fine and handsome—and the sweetest old gray-headed lady, and back of her two young women which I couldn't see right well. The old gentleman says:

"There; I reckon it's all right. Come in."

As soon as I was in the old gentleman he locked the door and barred it and bolted it, and told the young men to come in with their guns, and they all went in a big parlor that had a new rag carpet on the floor, and got together in a corner that was out of the range of the front windows—there warn't none on the side. They held the candle, and took a good look at me, and all said, "Why, *he* ain't a Shepherd-

son—no, there ain't any Shepherdson about him." Then
the old man said he hoped I wouldn't mind being searched
for arms, because he didn't mean no harm by it—it was only
to make sure. So he didn't pry into my pockets, but only felt
outside with his hands, and said it was all right. He told me to
make myself easy and at home, and tell all about myself; but
the old lady says:

"Why, bless you, Saul, the poor thing's as wet as he can
be; and don't you reckon it may be he's hungry?"

"True for you, Rachel—I forgot."

So the old lady says:

"Betsy" (this was a nigger woman), "you fly around and
get him something to eat as quick as you can, poor thing; and
one of you girls go and wake up Buck and tell him—oh,
here he is himself. Buck, take this little stranger and get the
wet clothes off from him and dress him up in some of yours
that's dry."

Buck looked about as old as me—thirteen or fourteen or
along there, though he was a little bigger than me. He hadn't
on anything but a shirt, and he was very frowzy-headed. He
came in gaping and digging one fist into his eyes, and he was
dragging a gun along with the other one. He says:

"Ain't they no Shepherdsons around?"

They said, no, 'twas a false alarm.

"Well," he says, "if they'd 'a' ben some, I reckon I'd 'a'
got one."

They all laughed, and Bob says:

"Why, Buck, they might have scalped us all, you've been
so slow in coming."

"Well, nobody come after me, and it ain't right. I'm
always kept down; I don't get no show."

"Never mind, Buck, my boy," says the old man, "you'll
have show enough, all in good time, don't you fret about

that. Go 'long with you now, and do as your mother told you."

When we got up-stairs to his room he got me a coarse shirt and a roundabout and pants of his, and I put them on. While I was at it he asked me what my name was, but before I could tell him he started to tell me about a bluejay and a young rabbit he had catched in the woods day before yesterday, and he asked me where Moses was when the candle went out. I said I didn't know; I hadn't heard about it before, no way.

"Well, guess," he says.

"How'm I going to guess," says I, "when I never heard tell of it before?"

"But you can guess, can't you? It's just as easy."

"Which candle?" I says.

"Why, any candle," he says.

"I don't know where he was," says I; "where was he?"

"Why, he was in the *dark!* That's where he was!"

"Well, if you knowed where he was, what did you ask me for?"

"Why, blame it, it's a riddle, don't you see? Say, how long are you going to stay here? You got to stay always. We can just have booming times—they don't have no school now. Do you own a dog? I've got a dog—and he'll go in the river and bring out chips that you throw in. Do you like to comb up Sundays, and all that kind of foolishness? You bet I don't, but ma she makes me. Confound these ole britches! I reckon I'd better put 'em on, but I'd ruther not, it's so warm. Are you all ready? All right. Come along, old hoss."

Cold corn-pone, cold corn-beef, butter and buttermilk—that is what they had for me down there, and there ain't nothing better that ever I've come across yet. Buck and his ma and all of them smoked cob pipes, except the nigger woman, which was gone, and the two young women. They all smoked and talked, and I eat and talked. The young women had quilts around them, and their hair down their backs. They all asked me questions, and I told them how pap and me and all the family was living on a little farm down at the bottom of Arkansaw, and my sister Mary Ann run off and got married and never was heard of no more, and Bill went to hunt them and he warn't heard of no more, and Tom and Mort died, and then there warn't nobody but just me and pap left, and he was just trimmed down to nothing, on account of his troubles; so when he died I took what there was left, because the farm didn't belong to us, and started up the river, deck passage, and fell overboard; and that was how I come to be here. So they said I could have a home there as long as I wanted it. Then it was most daylight and everybody went to bed, and I went to bed with Buck, and when I waked up in the morning, drat it all, I had forgot what my name was. So I laid there about an hour trying to think, and when Buck waked up I says:

"Can you spell, Buck?"

"Yes," he says.

"I bet you can't spell my name," says I.

"I bet you what you dare I can," says he.

"All right," says I, "go ahead."

"G-e-o-r-g-e J-a-x-o-n—there now," he says.

"Well," says I, "you done it, but I didn't think you could. It ain't no slouch of a name to spell—right off without studying."

I set it down, private, because somebody might want *me* to spell it next, and so I wanted to be handy with it and rattle it off like I was used to it.

It was a mighty nice family, and a mighty nice house, too. I hadn't seen no house out in the country before that was so nice and had so much style. It didn't have an iron latch on the front door, nor a wooden one with a buckskin string, but a brass knob to turn, the same as houses in town. There warn't no bed in the parlor, nor a sign of a bed; but heaps of parlors in towns has beds in them. There was a big fireplace that was bricked on the bottom, and the bricks was kept clean and red by pouring water on them and scrubbing them with another brick; sometimes they wash them over with red water-paint that they call Spanish-brown, same as they do in town. They had big brass dog-irons that could hold up a saw-log. There was a clock on the middle of the mantelpiece, with a picture of a town painted on the bottom half of the glass front, and a round place in the middle of it for the sun, and you could see the pendulum swinging behind it. It was beautiful to hear that clock tick; and sometimes when one of these peddlers had been along and scoured her up and got her in good shape, she would start in and strike a hundred and fifty before she got tuckered out. They wouldn't took any money for her.

Well, there was a big outlandish parrot on each side of the clock, made out of something like chalk, and painted up gaudy. By one of the parrots was a cat made of crockery, and a crockery dog by the other; and when you pressed down on them they squeaked, but didn't open their mouths nor look different nor interested. They squeaked through underneath. There was a couple of big wild-turkey-wing fans spread out behind those things. On the table in the middle of the room was a kind of a lovely crockery basket that had apples and oranges and peaches and grapes piled up in it, which was much redder and yellower and prettier than real ones is, but they warn't real because you could see where pieces had got chipped off and showed the white chalk, or whatever it was, underneath.

This table had a cover made out of a beautiful oilcloth, with a red and blue spread-eagle painted on it, and a painted border all around. It come all the way from Philadelphia, they said. There was some books, too, piled up perfectly exact, on each corner of the table. One was a big family Bible full of pictures. One was *Pilgrim's Progress,* about a man that left his family, it didn't say why. I read considerable in it now and then. The statements was interesting, but tough. Another was *Friendship's Offering,* full of beautiful stuff and poetry; but I didn't read the poetry. Another was Henry Clay's Speeches, and another was Dr. Gunn's *Family Medicine,* which told you all about what to do if a body was sick or dead. There was a hymn-book, and a lot of other books. And there was nice split-bottom chairs, and perfectly sound, too—not bagged down in the middle and busted, like an old basket.

They had pictures hung on the walls—mainly Washingtons and Lafayettes, and battles, and Highland Marys, and one called "Signing the Declaration." There was some that they called crayons, which one of the daughters which was dead made her own self when she was only fifteen years old. They was different from any pictures I ever seen before—blacker, mostly, than is common. One was a woman in slim black dress, belted small under the armpits, with bulges like a cabbage in the middle of the sleeves, and a large black scoop-shovel bonnet with a black veil, and white slim ankles crossed about with black tape, and very wee black slippers, like a chisel, and she was leaning pensive on a tombstone on her right elbow, under a weeping willow, and her other hand hanging down her side holding a white handkerchief and a reticule, and underneath the picture it said "Shall I Never See Thee More Alas." Another one was a young lady with her hair all combed up straight to the top of her head, and knotted there in front of a comb like a chair-back, and she was crying into a handkerchief and had a dead bird laying on its back in her other hand with its heels up, and underneath the picture it said "I Shall Never Hear Thy Sweet Chirrup More Alas." There was one where a young lady was at a window looking up at the moon, and tears running down her cheeks; and she had an open letter in one hand with black sealing-wax showing on one edge of it and she was mashing a locket with a chain to it against her mouth, and underneath the picture it said "And Art Thou Gone Yes Thou Art Gone Alas." These was all nice pictures, I reckon, but I didn't somehow seem to take to them, because if ever I was down a little they always give me the fan-tods. Everybody was sorry she died, because she had laid out a lot more of these pictures to do, and a body could see by what she had done what they had lost. But I reckoned that with her disposition she was having a better time in the graveyard. She was at work on what they said was her greatest picture when she took sick, and every day and every night it was her prayer to be allowed to live till she got it done, but she never got the chance. It was a picture of a young woman in a long white gown, standing on the rail of a bridge all ready to jump off, with her hair all down her back, and looking up to the moon, with the tears running down her face, and she had two arms folded across her breast, and two arms stretched out in front, and two more reaching up toward the moon—and the idea was to see which pair would look best and then scratch out all the other arms; but as I was saying, she died before she got her mind made up, and now they kept this picture over the head of the bed in her room, and every time her birthday come they hung flowers on it. Other times it was hid with a little curtain. The young woman in the picture had a kind of a nice sweet face, but there was so many arms it made her look too spidery, seemed to me.

This young girl kept a scrap-book when she was alive,

and used to paste obituaries and accidents and cases of patient suffering in it out of the *Presbyterian Observer,* and write poetry after them out of her own head. It was very good poetry. This is what she wrote about a boy by the name of Stephen Dowling Bots that fell down a well and was drownded:

ODE TO STEPHEN DOWLING BOTS, DEC'D

And did young Stephen sicken,
   And did young Stephen die?
And did the sad hearts thicken,
   And did the mourners cry?

No; such was not the fate of
   Young Stephen Dowling Bots;
Though sad hearts round him thickened,
   'Twas not from sickness' shots.

No whooping-cough did rack his frame,
   Nor measles drear with spots;
Not these impaired the sacred name
   Of Stephen Dowling Bots.

Despised love struck not with woe
   That head of curly knots,
Nor stomach troubles laid him low,
   Young Stephen Dowling Bots.

O no. Then list with tearful eye,
   Whilst I his fate do tell.

> His soul did from this cold world fly
>   By falling down a well.
>
> They got him out and emptied him;
>   Alas it was too late;
> His spirit was gone for to sport aloft
>   In the realms of the good and great.

If Emmeline Grangerford could make poetry like that before she was fourteen, there ain't no telling what she could 'a' done by and by. Buck said she could rattle off poetry like nothing. She didn't ever have to stop to think. He said she would slap down a line, and if she couldn't find anything to rhyme with it would just scratch it out and slap down another one, and go ahead. She warn't particular; she could write about anything you choose to give her to write about just so it was sadful. Every time a man died, or a woman died, or a child died, she would be on hand with her "tribute" before he was cold. She called them tributes. The neighbors said it was the doctor first, then Emmeline, then the undertaker—the undertaker never got in ahead of Emmeline but once, and then she hung fire on a rhyme for the dead person's name, which was Whistler. She warn't ever the same after that; she never complained, but she kinder pined away and did not live long. Poor thing, many's the time I made myself go up to the little room that used to be hers and get out her poor old scrap-book and read in it when her pictures had been aggravating me and I had soured on her a little. I liked all that family, dead ones and all, and warn't going to let anything come between us. Poor Emmeline made poetry about all the dead people when she was alive, and it didn't seem right that there warn't nobody to make some about her now she was gone; so I tried to sweat out a verse or two myself, but I couldn't seem to make it go somehow. They kept Emmeline's room trim and nice, and all the things fixed in it just the way she liked to have them when she was alive, and nobody ever slept there. The old lady took care of the room herself, though there was plenty of niggers, and she sewed there a good deal and read her Bible there mostly.

Well, as I was saying about the parlor, there was beautiful curtains on the windows; white, with pictures painted on them of castles with vines all down the walls, and cattle coming down to drink. There was a little old piano, too, that had tin pans in it, I reckon, and nothing was ever so lovely as to hear the young ladies sing "The Last Link is Broken" and play "The Battle of Prague" on it. The walls of all the rooms was plastered, and most had carpets on the floors, and the whole house was whitewashed on the outside.

It was a double house, and the big open place betwixt them was roofed and floored, and sometimes the table was set there in the middle of the day, and it was a cool, comfortable place. Nothing couldn't be better. And warn't the cooking good, and just bushels of it too!

CHAPTER XVIII

WHY HARNEY RODE AWAY FOR HIS HAT

COL. GRANGERFORD was a gentleman, you see. He was a gentleman all over; and so was his family. He was well born, as the saying is, and that's worth as much in a man as it is in a horse, so the Widow Douglas said, and nobody ever denied that she was of the first aristocracy in our town; and pap he always said it, too, though he warn't no more quality than a mudcat himself. Col. Grangerford was very tall and very slim, and had a darkish-paly complexion, not a sign of red in it anywheres; he was clean-shaved every morning all over his thin face, and he had the thinnest kind of lips, and the thinnest kind of nostrils, and a high nose, and heavy eyebrows, and the blackest kind of eyes, sunk so deep back that they seemed like they was looking out of caverns at you, as you may say. His forehead was high, and his hair was gray and straight and hung to his shoulders. His hands was long and thin, and every day of his life he put on a clean shirt and a full suit from head to foot made out of linen so white it hurt your eyes to look at it; and on Sundays he wore a blue tail-coat with brass buttons on it. He carried a mahogany cane with a silver head to it. There warn't no frivolishness about him, not a bit, and he warn't ever loud. He was as kind as he could be—you could feel that, you know, and so you had confidence. Sometimes he smiled, and it was good to see; but when he straightened himself up like a liberty-pole, and the lightning begun to flicker out from under his eyebrows, you wanted to climb a tree first, and find out what the matter was afterwards. He didn't ever have to tell anybody to mind their manners—everybody was always good-mannered where he was. Everybody loved to have him around, too; he was sunshine most always—I mean he made it seem like good weather. When he turned into a cloud-bank it was awful dark for half a minute, and that was enough; there wouldn't nothing go wrong again for a week.

When him and the old lady come down in the morning all the family got up out of their chairs and give them good day, and didn't set down again till they had set down. Then Tom and Bob went to the sideboard where the decanter was, and mixed a glass of bitters and handed it to him, and he held it in his hand and waited till Tom's and Bob's was mixed, and then they bowed and said, "Our duty to you, sir, and madam"; and *they* bowed the least bit in the world and said thank you, and so they drank, all three, and Bob and Tom poured a spoonful of water on the sugar and the mite of whisky or apple-brandy in the bottom of their tumblers, and give it to me and Buck, and we drank to the old people too.

Bob was the oldest and Tom next—tall, beautiful men with very broad shoulders and brown faces, and long black hair and black eyes. They dressed in white linen from head to foot, like the old gentleman, and wore broad Panama hats.

Then there was Miss Charlotte; she was twenty-five, and tall and proud and grand, but as good as she could be when she warn't stirred up; but when she was she had a look that would make you wilt in your tracks, like her father. She was beautiful.

So was her sister, Miss Sophia, but it was a different kind. She was gentle and sweet like a dove, and she was only twenty.

Each person had their own nigger to wait on them—Buck too. My nigger had a monstrous easy time, because I warn't used to having anybody to do anything for me, but Buck's was on the jump most of the time.

This was all there was of the family now, but there used to be more—three sons; they got killed; and Emmeline that died.

The old gentleman owned a lot of farms and over a hundred niggers. Sometimes a stack of people would come there, horseback, from ten or fifteen mile around, and stay five or six days, and have such junketings round about and on the river, and dances and picnics in the woods daytimes, and balls at the house nights. These people was mostly kin-folks of the family. The men brought their guns with them. It was a handsome lot of quality, I tell you.

There was another clan of aristocracy around there—five or six families—mostly of the name of Shepherdson. They was as high-toned and well born and rich and grand as the tribe of Grangerfords. The Shepherdsons and Grangerfords used the same steamboat-landing, which was about two mile above our house; so sometimes when I went up there with a lot of our folks I used to see a lot of the Shepherdsons there on their fine horses.

One day Buck and me was away out in the woods hunting, and heard a horse coming. We was crossing the road. Buck says:

"Quick! Jump for the woods!"

We done it, and then peeped down the woods through the leaves. Pretty soon a splendid young man came galloping down the road, setting his horse easy and looking like a soldier. He had his gun across his pommel. I had seen him before. It was young Harney Shepherdson. I heard Buck's gun go off at my ear, and Harney's hat tumbled off from his head. He grabbed his gun and rode straight to the place where we was hid. But we didn't wait. We started through the woods on a run. The woods warn't thick, so I looked over my shoulder to dodge the bullet, and twice I seen Harney cover Buck with his gun; and then he rode away the way he come—to get his hat, I reckon, but I couldn't see. We never stopped running till we got home. The old gentleman's eyes blazed a minute—'twas pleasure, mainly, I judged—then his face sort of smoothed down, and he says, kind of gentle:

"I don't like that shooting from behind a bush. Why didn't you step into the road, my boy?"

"The Shepherdsons don't, father. They always take advantage."

Miss Charlotte she held her head up like a queen while Buck was telling his tale, and her nostrils spread and her eyes snapped. The two young men looked dark, but never said nothing. Miss Sophia she turned pale, but the color came back when she found the man warn't hurt.

Soon as I could get Buck down by the corn-cribs under the trees by ourselves, I says:

"Did you want to kill him, Buck?"

"Well, I bet I did."

"What did he do to you?"

"Him? He never done nothing to me."

"Well, then, what did you want to kill him for?"

"Why, nothing—only it's on account of the feud."

"What's a feud?"

"Why, where was you raised? Don't you know what a feud is?"

"Never heard of it before—tell me about it."

"Well," says Buck, "a feud is this way: A man has a quarrel with another man, and kills him; then that other man's brother kills *him;* then the other brothers, on both sides, goes for one another; then the *cousins* chip in—and by and by everybody's killed off, and there ain't no more feud. But it's kind of slow, and takes a long time."

"Has this one been going on long, Buck?"

"Well, I should *reckon!* It started thirty year ago, or som'ers along there. There was trouble 'bout something, and then a lawsuit to settle it; and the suit went agin one of the men, and so he up and shot the man that won the suit—which he would naturally do, of course. Anybody would."

"What was the trouble about, Buck?—land?"

"I reckon maybe—I don't know."

"Well, who done the shooting? Was it a Grangerford or a Shepherdson?"

"Laws, how do *I* know? It was so long ago."

"Don't anybody know?"

"Oh, yes, pa knows, I reckon, and some of the other old people; but they don't know now what the row was about in the first place."

"Has there been many killed, Buck?"

"Yes; right smart chance of funerals. But they don't always kill. Pa's got a few buckshot in him; but he don't mind it 'cuz he don't weigh much, anyway. Bob's been carved up some with a bowie, and Tom's been hurt once or twice."

"Has anybody been killed this year, Buck?"

"Yes; we got one and they got one. 'Bout three months ago my cousin Bud, fourteen year old, was riding through the woods on t'other side of the river, and didn't have no weapon with him, which was blame' foolishness, and in a lonesome place he hears a horse a-coming behind him, and sees old Baldy Shepherdson a-linkin' after him with his gun in his hand and his white hair a-flying in the wind; and 'stead of jumping off and taking to the brush, Bud 'lowed he could outrun him; so they had it, nip and tuck, for five mile or more, the old man a-gaining all the time; so at last Bud seen it warn't any use, so he stopped and faced around so as to have the bullet-holes in front, you know, and the old man he rode up and shot him down. But he didn't git much chance to enjoy his luck, for inside of a week our folks laid *him* out."

"I reckon that old man was a coward, Buck."

"I reckon he *warn't* a coward. Not by a blame' sight. There ain't a coward amongst them Shepherdsons—not a one. And there ain't no cowards amongst the Grangerfords either. Why, that old man kep' up his end in the fight one day for half an hour against three Grangerfords, and come out winner. They was all a-horseback; he lit off of his horse and got behind a little woodpile, and kep' his horse before him to stop the bullets; but the Grangerfords stayed on their horses and capered around the old man, and peppered away at him, and he peppered away at them. Him and his horse both went home pretty leaky and crippled, but the Grangerfords had to be *fetched* home—and one of 'em was dead, and another died the next day. No, sir; if a body's out hunting for cowards he don't want to fool away any time amongst them Shepherdsons, becuz they don't breed any of that *kind*."

Next Sunday we all went to church, about three mile, everybody a-horseback. The men took their guns along, so did Buck, and kept them between their knees or stood them handy against the wall. The Shepherdsons done the same. It was pretty ornery preaching—all about brotherly love, and such-like tiresomeness; but everybody said it was a good sermon, and they all talked it over going home and had such a powerful lot to say about faith and good works and free grace and preforeordestination, and I don't know what all, that it did seem to me to be one of the roughest Sundays I had run across yet.

About an hour after dinner everybody was dozing around, some in their chairs and some in their rooms, and it got to be pretty dull. Buck and a dog was stretched out on the grass in the sun sound asleep. I went up to our room, and judged I would take a nap myself. I found that sweet Miss Sophia standing in her door, which was next to ours, and she took me in her room and shut the door very soft, and asked me if I liked her, and I said I did; and she asked me if I would do something for her and not tell anybody, and I said I would. Then she said she'd forgot her Testament, and left it in the seat at church between two other books, and would I slip out quiet and go there and fetch it to her, and not say nothing to nobody. I said I would. So I slid out and slipped off up the road, and there warn't anybody at the church, except maybe a hog or two, for there warn't any lock on the door, and hogs like a puncheon floor in summer-time because it's cool. If you notice, most folks don't go to church only when they've got to; but a hog is different.

Says I to myself, something's up; it ain't natural for a girl to be in such a sweat about a Testament. So I give it a shake, and out drops a little piece of paper with *"Half past two"* wrote on it with a pencil. I ransacked it, but couldn't find anything else. I couldn't make anything out of that, so I put the paper in the book again, and when I got home and upstairs there was Miss Sophia in her door waiting for me. She pulled me in and shut the door; then she looked in the Testament till she found the paper, and as soon as she read it she looked glad; and before a body could think she grabbed me and give me a squeeze, and said I was the best boy in the world, and not to tell anybody. She was mighty red in the face for a minute, and her eyes lighted up, and it made her powerful pretty. I was a good deal astonished, but when I got my breath I asked her what the paper was about, and she asked me if I had read it, and I said no, and she asked me if I could read writing, and I told her "no, only coarse-hand," and then she said the paper warn't anything but a book-mark to keep her place, and I might go and play now.

I went off down to the river, studying over this thing, and pretty soon I noticed that my nigger was following along behind. When we was out of sight of the house he

looked back and around a second, and then comes a-running,
and says:

"Mars Jawge, if you'll come down into de swamp I'll
show you a whole stack o' water-moccasins."

Thinks I, that's mighty curious; he said that yesterday. He
oughter know a body don't love water-moccasins enough to
go around hunting for them. What is he up to, anyway? So I
says:

"All right; trot ahead."

I followed a half a mile; then he struck out over the
swamp, and waded ankle-deep as much as another half-
mile. We come to a little flat piece of land which was dry and
very thick with trees and bushes, and he says:

"You shove right in dah jist a few steps, Mars Jawge;
dah's whah dey is. I's seed 'm befo'; I don't k'yer to see 'em
no mo'.'"

Then he slopped right along and went away, and pretty
soon the trees hid him. I poked into the place a ways and
come to a little open patch as big as a bedroom all hung
around with vines, and found a man laying there asleep—
and, by jings, it was my old Jim!

I waked him up, and I reckoned it was going to be a grand
surprise to him to see me again, but it warn't. He nearly
cried he was so glad, but he warn't surprised. Said he swum
along behind me that night, and heard me yell every time,
but dasn't answer, because he didn't want nobody to pick
him up and take him into slavery again. Says he:

"I got hurt a little, en couldn't swim fas', so I wuz a considerable ways behine you towards de las'; when you landed
I reck'ned I could ketch up wid you on de lan' 'dout havin' to
shout at you, but when I see dat house I begin to go slow. I
'uz off too fur to hear what dey say to you—I wuz 'fraid o'
de dogs; but when it 'uz all quiet ag'in I knowed you's in de

house, so I struck out for de woods to wait for day. Early in de mawnin' some er de niggers come along, gwyne to de fields, en dey tuk me en showed me dis place, whah de dogs can't track me on account o' de water, en dey brings me truck to eat every night, en tells me how you's a-gittin' along."

"Why didn't you tell my Jack to fetch me sooner?"

"Well, 'twarn't no use to 'sturb you, Huck, tell we could do sumfn. I ben a-buyin' pots en pans en vittles, as I got a chanst, en a-patchin' up de raf' nights when—"

"What raft, Jim?"

"Our ole raf'."

"You mean to say our old raft warn't smashed all to flinders?"

"No, she warn't. She was tore up a good deal—one en' of her was; but dey warn't no great harm done, on'y our traps was mos' all los'. Ef we hadn' dive' so deep en swum so fur under water, en de night hadn't ben so dark, en we warn't so sk'yerd, en ben sich punkinheads, as de sayin' is, we'd a seed de raf'. But it's jis' as well we didn't, 'kase now she's all fixed up ag'in mos' as good as new, en we's got a new lot o' stuff, in de place o' what 'uz los'."

"Why, how did you get hold of the raft again, Jim—did you catch her?"

"How I gwyne to ketch her en I out in de woods? No; some er de niggers foun' her ketched on a snag along heah in de ben', en dey hid her in a crick 'mongst de willows, en dey wuz so much jawin' 'bout which un 'um she b'long to de mos' dat I come to heah 'bout it pooty soon, so I ups en settles de trouble by tellin' 'um she don't b'long to none uv 'um, but to you en me; en I ast 'm if dey gwyne to grab a young white genlman's propaty, en git a hid'n for it? Den I gin 'm ten cents apiece, en dey 'uz mighty well satisfied, en wisht some mo' raf's 'ud come along en make 'm rich ag'in. Dey's mighty good to me, dese niggers is, en whatever I wants 'm to do fur me I doan' have to ast 'm twice, honey. Dat Jack's a good nigger, en pooty smart."

"Yes, he is. He ain't ever told me you was here; told me to come, and he'd show me a lot of water-moccasins. If anything happens *he* ain't mixed up in it. He can say he never seen us together, and it 'll be the truth."

I don't want to talk much about the next day. I reckon I'll cut it pretty short. I waked up about dawn, and was a-going to turn over and go to sleep again when I noticed how still it was—didn't seem to be anybody stirring. That warn't usual. Next I noticed that Buck was up and gone. Well, I gets up, a-wondering, and goes down-stairs—everything as still as a mouse. Just the same outside. Thinks I, what does it mean? Down by the woodpile I comes across my Jack, and says:

"What's it all about?"

Says he:

"Don't you know, Mars Jawge?"

"No," says I, "I don't."

"Well, den, Miss Sophia's run off! 'deed she has. She run off in de night some time—nobody don't know jis' when; run off to get married to dat young Harney Shepherdson, you know—leastways, so dey 'spec. De fambly foun' it out 'bout half an hour ago—maybe a little mo'—en' I *tell* you dey warn't no time los'. Sich another hurryin' up guns en hosses *you* never see! De women folks has gone for to stir up de relations, en ole Mars Saul en de boys tuck dey guns en rode up de river road for to try to ketch dat young man en kill him 'fo' he kin git acrost de river wid Miss Sophia. I reck'n dey's gwyne to be mighty rough times."

"Buck went off 'thout waking me up."

"Well, I reck'n he *did*! Dey warn't gwyne to mix you up

in it. Mars Buck he loaded up his gun en 'lowed he's gwyne to fetch home a Shepherdson or bust. Well, dey'll be plenty un 'm dah, I reck'n, en you bet you he'll fetch one ef he gits a chanst."

I took up the river road as hard as I could put. By and by I begin to hear guns a good ways off. When I came in sight of the log store and the woodpile where the steamboats lands I worked along under the trees and brush till I got to a good place, and then I clumb up into the forks of a cotton-wood that was out of reach, and watched. There was a wood-rank four foot high a little ways in front of the tree, and first I was going to hide behind that; but maybe it was luckier I didn't.

There was four or five men cavorting around on their horses in the open place before the log store, cussing and yelling, and trying to get at a couple of young chaps that was behind the wood-rank alongside of the steamboat-landing; but they couldn't come it. Every time one of them showed himself on the river side of the woodpile he got shot at. The two boys was squatting back to back behind the pile, so they could watch both ways.

By and by the men stopped cavorting around and yelling. They started riding towards the store; then up gets one of the boys, draws a steady bead over the woodrank, and drops one of them out of his saddle. All the men jumped off of their horses and grabbed the hurt one and started to carry him to the store; and that minute the two boys started on the run. They got half-way to the tree I was in before the men noticed. Then the men see them, and jumped on their horses and took out after them. They gained on the boys, but it didn't do no good, the boys had too good a start; they got to the woodpile that was in front of my tree, and slipped in behind it, and so they had the bulge on the men again.

One of the boys was Buck, and the other was a slim young chap about nineteen years old.

The men ripped around awhile, and then rode away. As soon as they was out of sight I sung out to Buck and told him. He didn't know what to make of my voice coming out of the tree at first. He was awful surprised. He told me to watch out sharp and let him know when the men come in sight again; said they was up to some devilment or other—wouldn't be gone long. I wished I was out of that tree, but I dasn't come down. Buck begun to cry and rip, and 'lowed that him and his cousin Joe (that was the other young chap) would make up for this day yet. He said his father and his two brothers was killed, and two or three of the enemy. Said the Shepherdsons laid for them in ambush. Buck said his father and brothers ought to waited for their relations—the Shepherdsons was too strong for them. I asked him what was become of young Harney and Miss Sophia. He said they'd got across the river and was safe. I was glad of that; but the way Buck did take on because he didn't manage to kill Harney that day he shot at him—I hain't ever heard anything like it.

All of a sudden, bang! bang! bang! goes three or four guns—the men had slipped around through the woods and come in from behind without their horses! The boys jumped for the river—both of them hurt—and as they swum down the current the men run along the bank shooting at them and singing out, "Kill them, kill them!" It made me so sick I most fell out of the tree. I ain't a-going to tell *all* that happened—it would make me sick again if I was to do that. I wished I hadn't ever come ashore that night to see such things. I ain't ever going to get shut of them—lots of times I dream about them.

I stayed in the tree till it begun to get dark, afraid to come down. Sometimes I heard guns away off in the woods; and twice I seen little gangs of men gallop past the log store with guns; so I reckoned the trouble was still a-going on. I was mighty down hearted; so I made up my mind I wouldn't ever go anear that house again, because I reckoned I was to blame, somehow. I judged that that piece of paper meant that Miss Sophia was to meet Harney somewheres at half past two and run off; and I judged I ought to told her father about that paper and the curious way she acted, and then maybe he would 'a' locked her up, and this mess wouldn't happen.

When I got down out of the tree I crept along down the river-bank a piece and found the two bodies laying in the edge of the water, and tugged at them till I got them ashore; then I covered up their faces, and got away as quick as I could. I cried a little when I was covering up Buck's face, for he was mighty good to me.

It was just dark now. I never went near the house, but struck through the woods and made for the swamp. Jim warn't on his island, so I tramped off in a hurry for the crick, and crowded through the willows, red-hot to jump aboard and get out of that awful country. The raft was gone! My souls, but I was scared! I couldn't get my breath for most a minute. Then I raised a yell. A voice not twenty-five foot from me says:

"Good lan'! is dat you, honey? Doan' make no noise."

It was Jim's voice—nothing ever sounded so good before. I run along the bank a piece and got aboard, and Jim he grabbed me and hugged me, he was so glad to see me. He says:

"Laws bless you, chile, I 'uz right down sho' you's dead ag'in. Jack's been heah; he says he reck'n you's ben shot, kase you didn' come home no mo'; so I's jes' dis minute a-startin' de raf' down towards de mouf er de crick, so's to be all ready for to shove out en leave soon as Jack comes ag'in en tells me for certain you *is* dead. Lawsy, I's mighty glad to git you back ag'in, honey."

"All right—that's mighty good; they won't find me, and they'll think I've been killed, and floated down the river— there's something up there that 'll help them think so—so don't you lose no time, Jim, but just shove off for the big water as fast as ever you can."

I never felt easy till the raft was two mile below there and out in the middle of the Mississippi. Then we hung up our signal lantern, and judged that we was free and safe once more. I hadn't had a bite to eat since yesterday, so Jim he got out some corn-dodgers and buttermilk, and pork and cabbage and greens—there ain't nothing in the world so good when it's cooked right—and whilst I eat my supper we talked and had a good time. I was powerful glad to get away from the feuds, and so was Jim to get away from the swamp. We said there warn't no home like a raft, after all. Other places do seem so cramped up and smothery, but a raft don't. You feel mighty free and easy and comfortable on a raft.

ELEMENTS OF SHARED INQUIRY
A Short Course On
Interpretive Reading
And Discussion

PART TWO

TEXTUAL ANALYSIS

Even if you have a good memory, you have probably found it necessary during the discussion to read some passage again either to answer a question about it or to check the soundness of someone else's answer. These are good reasons for always having the selection you are discussing right in front of you. Another is that having the selection there gives you a chance to do textual analysis. By textual analysis, we mean a detailed examination of a particular passage in which you try to determine the author's meaning line by line and sometimes word by word.

This activity may be carried on as a way of getting into a selection when the group has not read it well enough to explore an interpretive question. Textual analysis is also valuable when a group is interpreting a work satisfactorily and has a number of ideas about what a work means. In this situation, textual analysis is a way of using the ideas already expressed to extract more meaning from particular passages, meanings that may help to answer an interpretive question satisfactorily.

Step A. Find the passage that you want to examine closely and have someone in the group read it aloud. Even if it is difficult, you may get some new sense of what it is about.

Step B. Identify who is talking. It may be the author speaking to you directly, a fictitious narrator, or one of the characters speaking to another character.

Step C. If you choose some passage other than the beginning, try to get a rough idea of where you are in the selection. Look briefly at the page or two before the passage to help refresh your memory.

Step D. This step is the most important one. Go over the difficult passage, line by line. Ask any questions about the meaning of words, phrases, and sentences to which you are not sure of the answer. If you are called on to answer questions that someone else has about a line, try to put your response into your own words instead of using the words of the author. If you simply repeat what the author says, you may not really understand his meaning. Feel free to turn to other sections of the work that you think will help you answer questions about the passage you are examining closely. No one can tell you specifically what passages to turn to, but they are usually passages dealing with the same ideas, often expressed in the same words.

EXERCISE 6
"The Evildoer"

To find out how textual analysis works, see how many questions you can ask and answer for the following passage from "The Evildoer." We have suggested a few questions. See whether you can think of others.

"So, you state that you unscrewed this nut in order to use it as a sinker?"

"What else? Not to play knucklebones with!"

"But you could have used a piece of lead, or a bullet, or some kind of nail ... "

"You don't find lead lying around to be picked up, you have to buy it, and a nail's no good. There's nothing better than a nut. It's heavy and it's got a hole."

"He keeps acting the fool! You might think he was born yesterday or dropped out of the sky! Can't you get it through your thick skull what all this unscrewing can lead to? If not for the watchman, the train might have gone off the rails, people might have been killed! You would have killed these people."

"God forbid, Your Honor! Why would I want to kill people? Am I not a Christian—am I some kind of criminal? Praise be to God, my good sir, I've lived all my life not only without killing but without even thinking of such a thing. Save us and have mercy upon us, Queen of Heaven!—how can you even say such a thing?"

"And, according to you, what causes train wrecks? Unscrew two or three nuts and you'll have a train wreck!"

1. Who makes the opening statement?

2. Why has the peasant been brought before the judge?

3. Why does the judge find it so hard to believe that the peasant uses the nut in fishing?

4. Why does the peasant keep talking about the purpose of the nut rather than about how he obtained it?

5. Why does the judge suggest alternative things the peasant might have used for sinkers?

6. Why is the statement of the judge after "some kind of nail . . . "broken off?

7. Why does the author have the peasant come up quickly with reasons why other objects are not suitable as sinkers?

8. Does the author want us to agree with the judge that the peasant is acting like a fool?

9. Does the author want us to agree with the judge that what the peasant did could cause a train wreck?

10. Why is the peasant horrified at the suggestion that what he has done is criminal?

11. Why does the judge now talk about the danger of unscrewing two or three nuts?

12. Does the author want us to believe both the peasant and the judge are right from their standpoints?

PUTTING GUESSES ABOUT MEANING INTO YOUR INTERPRETIVE QUESTIONS

Sometimes you may have your own guess about the author's meaning, and you would like to hear what other members of the group think of it. As long as you believe there are arguments for and against it, you are free to include it in your interpretive question. For example, after reading "Rufus," you may think that Rufus is trying to conduct himself with the boys in a way that his father would approve of. The question might then be: Does Rufus act the way he does with the boys to make his father proud of him?

Since our aim in shared inquiry is to get participants to think for themselves about what a selection means, we encourage you to write questions that share your best thinking with the group. Besides, you sometimes have to put your own guess about the author's meaning into your question if you are going to be honest about the problem of interpretation you want to explore. For example, if we had asked, "Why does Rufus act the way he does with the boys?" we would have left out something important to us in the question. We would have left out our guess that Rufus is trying to act with the boys in the way his father told him to.

Including guesses about meaning can help you to write better questions, too. Take the question: How does the author tell his story? As worded, it could be answered factually "He tells the story from the viewpoint of Rufus" and, with no word change, it could be asked about any story. Putting a guess about meaning into the question makes it clearly interpretive and specific: Why does the author tell the story through the mind and eyes of Rufus?

Although you are free, in shared inquiry, to put any guesses

173

you like into your interpretive questions, you should never indicate how you would answer a question. We call questions that tell people the answers you expect "leading" questions. Usually, there is some word in a leading question that lets you know what answer is expected. It may be an adverb such as "really" or "truly." Example: Does Rufus *really* believe his father's soul can see him? Or the use of a negative word instead of a more neutral one. Example: *Doesn't* Rufus have mixed feelings about his father's death because of his age? Sometimes you can improve a leading question by merely dropping the telltale word: Does Rufus have mixed feelings about his father's death because of his age? Other times, the question can be improved by including in it some guess you have about the author's meaning: Does Rufus think his father's soul is watching him because he feels guilty? If a leading question can't be easily revised, it should be dropped.

EXERCISE 7
"Rufus"

Some of the questions below are good interpretive questions and others are "leading" questions that suggest pretty clearly how the person wants the question answered. Place an (I) before each interpretive question and an (L) before each leading question.

_____ 1. Does the author really want us to believe Rufus has been bad in the story?

_____ 2. Why does one stranger act as if he doesn't hear when Rufus says, "My daddy's dead"?

_____ 3. Does it actually make any difference how Rufus's father was killed?

_____ 4. Does the author believe adults, as well as children, don't know how to act when someone dies?

_____ 5. Why does Rufus think of the word "concussion" after his conversation with the boys?

_____ 6. Isn't the way Catherine colors supposed to suggest that she is disturbed about her father's death?

_____ 7. Why is Rufus only able to accept the fact that his father is dead toward the end of the story?

_____ 8. Does the author think deep grief is too personal for another person to understand?

_____ 9. Why does Rufus lick the ashes from his father's ashtray?

_____ 10. Doesn't Rufus "show off" because the boys had always teased him in the past?

INTERPRETIVE QUESTIONS IN THE
FORM OF ISSUES

Quite apart from shared inquiry, we often talk about "issues." We find issues in the news, we argue about issues, and we agree or disagree with a political leader's stand on issues. In this sense, the word is used to describe any controversial problem about which people have different and usually opposite views. In shared inquiry, the word has a similar but more specialized meaning: an "issue" is an interpretive question that includes a guess about the author's meaning and that calls for alternative answers, one or both of which may turn out to be correct.

An issue may be an interpretive question that you can answer with either a "Yes" or "No." For example: Does the author believe Uncle Oscar, as well as Paul's mother, is responsible for Paul's death? An issue may also be an interpretive question that requires you to choose between alternative ideas: Does the author have Paul die 1) to show that he was willing to sacrifice himself for his mother *or* 2) to make her realize what she had done?

As with all interpretive questions, you must back up your answer to a question in the form of an issue. You must show, with evidence from the story, why you decided on the "Yes" or "No" or why you chose one idea instead of the other. It is the support you present for either side of the issue that can increase our understanding of the selection.

An interpretive question in the form of an issue always contains a guess about the author's meaning. In our "Yes" and "No" question the guess is: The author may want us to believe Uncle Oscar, as well as Paul's mother, is responsible for Paul's death. In the question with alternatives there are two guesses: 1) the author may have Paul die to show how far he is willing to go to make his mother happy *or* 2) the author may use Paul's death to make his mother realize what her greed has led to.

Since many interpretive questions lead to alternative or opposing answers, you may wonder why we call your attention to questions in the form of issues. One reason is that issues are an excellent way to make the group immediately aware that a question can be answered correctly in more than one way. Often we don't realize this as quickly when we ask an interpretive question that does not contain a guess about the author's meaning. For example: Why does the author have Paul ride a rocking-horse to find luck?

A second reason is that a question in the form of an issue is a good way to interest someone in a problem of interpretation. In this respect, questions as issues serve much the same purpose in shared inquiry that they serve in debate. They dramatize a problem by making people wonder which side will have the stronger case. In another respect, however, issues in shared inquiry differ from issues in debate. Our interest is not primarily in proving one side right and the other side wrong or in having someone stick to the side he first thinks is right, even though he changes his mind later. Often, participants discover that the turth about the author's meaning consists of good ideas from both sides. Nevertheless, the issue has served its purpose if it captures the attention of the participants who are discussing it.

When you try to write questions in the form of issues there are three mistakes that are easy to make. The first is to present an issue that really can't be answered in two opposing ways if you have read the whole selection carefully. For example: Does Paul finally realize he is not a lucky person? The question is an issue only for someone who has not finished the selection or has read it carelessly.

A second mistake is to present an issue that possibly can be answered in two ways but almost all of the evidence from the selection is on one side. For us such a question would be: "Does the author want us to believe Paul enjoys his gift for picking winners?" Although, at one point, Bassett says Paul takes pleasure in betting, throughout most of the story Paul is in a state of torment or agony until he "knows" the horse who will win.

A final mistake is to make an issue out of the group's beliefs instead of the author's meaning—in other words to ask an evaluation question instead of an interpretive one. Example: Did you like Bassett?

To avoid all the mistakes we have mentioned, remember that an issue is satisfactory in shared inquiry only when you think it can be answered in opposing or alternative ways based on a careful reading of the whole selection.

EXERCISE 8
"The Rocking-Horse Winner"

Place an (Is) next to each question that is in the form of an issue. These are *interpretive* questions that call for alternative answers based on a careful reading of the story. Place an (X) next to each question that is not an issue. Hint: All good interpretive questions are *not* issues.

_____ 1. Does the author have Paul confuse "luck" and "lucre" because he thinks they are both evil?

_____ 2. Does the author have the house whisper to show us or to help prepare us for the magic of the horse?

_____ 3. Do you believe being happy depends on luck?

_____ 4. Does the author agree with Paul that he is a lucky boy?

_____ 5. Why doesn't the rocking-horse have a name?

_____ 6. Is Paul's mother solely responsible for the house whispering?

_____ 7. Would Paul's mother have stopped him if she had known about his gambling?

_____ 8. Why does the author have Paul's mother come from a gambling family?

_____ 9. Does Paul's mother work secretly for the same reason Paul rides his horse secretly?

_____ 10. Does the author want us to think less of Bassett because he wins money on Paul's last trip?

INTERPRETIVE QUESTIONS ABOUT THE ORGANIZATION OF A STORY

When you write interpretive questions, it is easy to forget that a story has an author, a person who made it up and put it all together in a certain way. Often you ask questions about why a character acted in a certain way or why something happened in a particular situation, just as you might ask about characters or actions in real life. However, there is another form of interpretive question you can ask about the author's meaning—one that requires someone to think about why the author decided to tell the story in the way that he or she did. We call interpretive questions that remind you that the story is "made up," questions of organization.

You can ask questions of organization about many different things in a story. You might ask someone to consider why the story takes place when it does or where it does. For example: Why is "The Zodiacs" about seventh graders instead of, say, about boys in high school? Or you might ask a fellow participant to explain why certain scenes appear in a particular order, or why they are in the story at all. For instance: Why does the author have George humiliated by the cop before Louie tries to get George to pitch for the Zodiacs again?

Still other organizational questions can make you conscious of the point of view from which a story is told. For example: Why does the author choose to tell his story through a narrator who is looking back at an earlier experience? Questions about organization may also encourage you to explore the reason the author gives a character certain qualities or has that character act in a particular way. Example: Why did the author make Louie the worst athlete and the smartest kid in the class?

181

What all these examples of questions about organization have in common is that they make you think about how the story is written rather than about what happens in the story. They make you think about things the character does not control or the use that the author makes of a character. They also make you think about the pattern of the story—the part that scenes or events may play in the author's design or plan.

There are three mistakes you should avoid in trying to write questions about the organization of a story. The first is asking an evaluative question instead of an interpretive one. For example: Did you want George to rejoin the team? Our emotional reactions to what we are reading can be an important way of alerting us to questions about how the author wrote the story in the way that he or she did, such as: Why does the author have George rejoin the team? but we don't want to ask evaluative questions that do little more than poll the feelings of the group.

A second mistake to be avoided is writing questions about the organization of a story that are too general. For example: Why does the author end the story in the way he does? You could ask similar questions about any story. The way to improve such questions is to think more about what the problem of organization is for you in this story. A more specific version of the last question for us would be: Why does the author want us to know George quit school and probably took off with his gangster brother?

The last mistake to watch for in writing questions of organization is the hardest one to avoid. It is confusing a question about *why a character acts* in a certain way with a question about *why the author has the character act* in that way. As long as the question could be answered without thinking about the author's purpose, it is *not* a question of organization. For example: Why is Louie willing to let George keep four of the twelve dollars he stole if he'll play with the team?

As you may have noticed, the mistakes in writing questions about organization are not new ones. They are some of the same difficulties we always run into when we are trying to write good interpretive questions: we substitute questions of evaluation for questions of interpretation; questions are not specific enough; or the wording of our question does not clearly indicate what we want to discuss.

EXERCISE 9
"The Zodiacs"

Place an (O) next to each question that is satisfactory as a question about the organization of the story and an (X) next to each question that is not. Remember, if the question is evaluative, not specific, or is really about the action of a character, then it is not satisfactory as an organizational question.

_____ 1. Why does the author make George's brother a coward?

_____ 2. Why is George made a year older than the other boys and a member of a tough gang?

_____ 3. Would you have let George keep some of the money he stole to get him back on the team?

_____ 4. Why does George steal the raffle money?

_____ 5. Why is the story written so that George and Louie are needed to make the team a success?

_____ 6. Why does the narrator mention that he kept the clipping about his team until his third year of high school?

_____ 7. Why does the author show us Louie crying?

_____ 8. Why is there one other boy besides George whose raffle account isn't correct?

_____ 9. Why does George show up with his gang after the game?

_____ 10. Why is there a great deal of dialog in the story?

FOLLOW-UP QUESTIONS

To explore an interpretive question successfully in discussion, you must use follow-up questions. These are all the questions the leaders or participants ask after the interpretive question for discussion has been stated. The purpose of follow-up questions is to encourage you and all participants to think for yourselves and, at the same time, to use what is said to keep the discussion moving until the interpretive question is answered, or time runs out.

This is not easy to do. Some participants talk so fast that it is hard to think about what they are saying. At times, you will hear more ideas than you can possibly think about, and at other times, no one will have anything to say. Ideas are often expressed in ways that are not immediately clear. You will discover that some of your fellow participants are quicker to offer opinions than to support them with facts, and sometimes the facts they do offer are incorrect. Some participants will talk about topics not related to the interpretive question or even to the selection; and you may from time to time lose your own train of thought. The effective use of follow-up questions by the discussion leaders—and by you as a participant—will help to handle all these situations and to keep the group's attention on the interpretive question.

Follow-up questions have four uses: to get participants to answer interpretive questions; to clarify their answers; to ask participants to support their opinions with facts; and to keep discussion on the track.

1. When a participant fails to answer an opening interpretive question or any interpretive question, the discussion leaders may repeat the question or rephrase it. They may direct the repeated or rephrased question either to the

participant who failed to respond or to someone else. Another way the discussion leaders may handle a lack of response is to ask a factual or evaluative question that may give you some ideas that will help you to answer their interpretive question. Question: Sally, In "Univac to Univac," why does the poet want to show how human beings might look to computers? Answer: I don't know. Factual question: Sally, What does the computer criticize about human beings? Or Evaluative question: What faults do you find in people? Follow-up questions are also asked to get more than one answer to an interpretive question. Examples: Alice, do you agree with Ted? Bob, how would you answer the questions? Fran, what do you think? Even when it turns out that two participants have the same interpretation, asking for additional opinions is not wasted. The second participant often produces new facts to support the opinion.

2. The second use of follow-up questions is to clarify answers. The discussion leaders and the participants should ask for clarification of any response that they don't understand. You can almost always be sure that if *you* don't understand what is said, at least some other members of the group don't either. One way to get clarification is to ask the participant to repeat what he or she said in different words. Examples: Sally, could you restate that? Frank, what did you mean by that? Another way is to state in your own words what you *think* the participant means and ask him or her if you are correct. Example: John, are you saying that the poet wants us to value many of the things about human beings that the computer criticizes?

3. The third use of follow-up questions is to ask participants to support their opinions with facts. This is done

by asking factual questions that require participants to read from the selection or to put what the author said into their own words. Examples: Where do you see that in the story? What evidence can you find in the story for that statement? Everyone has a right to an opinion, but what makes some opinions better than others is the way they are backed up with evidence from the story.

4. The final use of follow-up questions is to keep discussion on the track. It takes a great deal of concentration on the part of both leaders and participants to stick to the interpretive problem being discussed. Therefore, it is not uncommon to find participants and leaders occasionally wandering into other areas of discussion about either the selection or their personal experience. The solution in both cases is to ask interpretive or factual questions that bring the group back to the problem of meaning which they are supposed to be discussing. Example: Does the poet believe human beings should do just the opposite of what the computer wants—organize to stamp out mechanical activities? Answer: I think we need machines. They make life easier. Question: But in the poem, does the author approve of Mark I and Mark II not doing what the machine tells them to?

EXERCISE 10
"The Companion"

Each sequence below consists of a question and an answer. After each response, write one follow-up question. Your question should continue the discussion of the story by taking into account the participant's answer *and* the leader's question.

1. Leader: Why does the narrator call the girl "she," "child," "girl," "companion," and "Katya," in the poem?

   Participant: Because he sees her in different ways.
   Your question: _____

2. Leader: Why does the narrator say, "I even whistled"?

   Participant: To show he wasn't afraid.
   Your question: _____

3. Leader: Does the poet suggest that neither the girl nor the boy could have made it without the other?

   Participant: No, the girl could have made it without the boy. She has food, is well dressed for walking, and proves to be strong.
   Your question: _____

4. Leader: Why does the narrator have such a superior attitude towards girls at the beginning of the poem?

   Participant: He hasn't had much to do with them.
   Your question: _____

5. Leader: Why does the poet suggest it is spring?
   Participant: There's no indication of the season of the
                    year. All we know is that it is 1941.
   Your question: _____
6. Leader: Why does the poet tell us the girl looks
                    helpless before he tells us her age?
   Participant: The poet wants us to see the girl as the
                    narrator does. The first thing he notices is
                    how helpless she is. Only when he starts
                    to talk to her does he learn her age.
   Your question: _____

RESOLUTION IN SHARED INQUIRY

In shared inquiry, the word "resolution" means more than getting the right answer to a question.

Resolution is that point in a discussion when all the members of your group could, if called upon, (1) answer the interpretive question on which the discussion is based in their own way, and (2) support their answers with facts from the selection. Since interpretive questions can usually be answered satisfactorily in more than one way, it is likely that members of the group will have different answers.

You can see from this definition that resolution does not mean total agreement or even a majority opinion about an answer. Resolution is an individual matter. *It occurs when you are convinced that the way in which you would answer an interpretive question can be supported with evidence that satisifies you.* If you were the discussion leader, you should continue to explore the interpretive question at least until you could make up your own mind about how the question should be answered. As a participant, you should feel free to bring up points about an interpretive question as long as you have any doubt about how *you* would answer it.

One reliable sign that the group is leaving an interpretive question before everyone has resolved it to his or her satisfaction is the attempt of a participant to reintroduce it if the leaders switch to another question about the author's meaning. If that occurs, your discussion leaders should backtrack for a moment or two to determine whether new facts or ideas are being raised that could provide another answer to the question you are discussing.

There are also signs to show that you are approaching the resolution of an interpretive question or that it probably will not be worthwhile to continue the discussion of it much longer: the group begins to repeat itself, to take up minor points, and to wander away from the question. When that happens the group has probably run out of ideas that further the exploration of the interpretive question on which this segment of your discussion is based.

Because resolution depends so much on what the leaders and the participants do, the same interpretive question might be answered differently by different groups. Your group might answer the question, "Why did Huck have a conflict about turning Jim in?", by talking about Huck's growing feeling of respect and affection for Jim, the values of the society in which Huck was brought up, and Jim's faith in Huck. Another group might have answers to the same question that never occurred to your group. They might mention how Huck's conscience tells him he ought to turn Jim in, whereas his feelings tell him he ought to help Jim; they might also discuss Huck's realization that no matter what he did he would feel bad.

Although your group should try to resolve in its own way every interpretive question they are discussing before proceeding to the next one, the success of shared inquiry does not depend wholly on whether you do or not. You can increase your understanding of a selection even if you feel more could be said in answer to some interpretive questions. You can also experience with each interpretive question the pleasure of thinking for yourself.

EXERCISE 11
"Huckleberry Finn"

The purpose of this exercise is to illustrate what we mean by resolution, and to test our statement that resolution of an interpretive question will be different for different groups. Your discussion leaders will divide you into two or three small groups and ask a member of each group to list all the topics or ideas you would have to discuss to answer the question:

Why does the author have Huck stop his trip down the river to stay with the Grangerfords?